A CONTEMPORARY CHRISTIAN ROMANCE NOVELLA

Now or Never

EMILY CONRAD

1

————

"You're lucky you're dying." Tim's daughter slammed the SUV's door to punctuate her declaration.

"About that ..." Even alone in the vehicle, Tim couldn't bring himself to voice the latest development.

You're lucky you're dying.

Isabella's statement burrowed deep and promised to fester. At twenty-three, she should've outgrown such theatrics. Then again, she *was* an actress, and he hadn't shared the results of his biopsy. What was he, a fifty-two-year-old, doing keeping secrets?

Grasping at straws, that was what. If he'd told Isabella about his great prognosis, she wouldn't have come on this trip and how would he ever connect with her?

Her locks shimmered under the blazing Iowa sun as she stalked up the wide concrete steps and into the brick building. She'd inherited his blond hair, though the thick texture was a gift from her mother. The first day of their trip, she'd worn shorts so short he'd seen swimming suits with better coverage. Since then, he'd been cranking the air conditioning. The strategy had worked; she'd paired today's cropped top with full-length jeans. She slung open the door and disappeared inside like she owned the restaurant, though that distinction went to a former client of his named Philip Miller.

He breathed a long sigh. For all Tim's mistakes, at least he'd succeeded at raising an independent woman. If only he didn't have to watch her use that strength to brazenly repeat his worst choices.

To think this road trip was supposed to bring them closer.

He swiped his hand down his face and prayed for wisdom. Asking God for help in moments like these was finally coming more naturally to him after becoming a believer eight years before. He pushed open the door, and heat waving off the fresh asphalt swamped him as he stepped out of the vehicle. Above the entrance, a vintage-looking marquee sign labeled the business The Depot and promised food, drinks, and music.

The music part had prompted the trouble with Issy—no, Isabella. She'd been asking him to drop the nickname since age thirteen. A decade later, he shouldn't keep slipping. He had to do better. He *would* do better.

Inside, the dining area occupied the front third of the converted train station. Then came the bar, situated to serve diners and those attending shows in the hall beyond. Shadows shrouded the event space.

Given the small size of Many Oaks, Iowa, and the time—midafternoon—a surprising number of patrons occupied the wooden tables and chairs. With brick walls, penny-colored floor tiles, and tall ceilings, voices and scraping chairs echoed. He could only imagine how loud the trains must've been. Hopefully Philip had ensured better acoustics in the hall beyond.

Laughter rang out from a booth along the left wall. Philip appeared to be in the middle of a story, gesturing over empty plates that littered the table. His audience included a clean-cut guy in his twenties and a striking woman older than Philip, closer to Tim's age. Another guy stood next to the booth, dressed in all black like a stagehand. Since Philip had made the same color choice—all black—perhaps it was the restaurant's employee dress code.

The woman seated across from Philip glanced toward Tim. Her hair was down but swept back from her face, showing off striking cheekbones and expressive eyebrows. She had the looks of a Broadway star. He would know after three trips to attend the musical Issy—Isabella—had performed in during its year-long run.

Speaking of Isabella, he ought to quit gawking and find her.

But it was too late. Philip abandoned the booth and started toward him. "How was the drive?"

Tim returned a loose hug. "Uneventful until the end."

As Philip stepped back, humor played across his face. "Things got interesting when you reached Many Oaks? That's unusual."

"I bet." The town was an oasis in a desert of cornfields. GPS had routed them through the town square, where old brick buildings surrounded a park. The country had smaller towns, but did it get any quainter?

Philip's gaze flicked past him then back.

Tim pivoted and spotted Isabella in a booth. A waiter leaned against the side of the bench facing her, engrossed in conversation.

That was quick.

Then again, Tim had blinked and Isabella had shot up about a foot and gained curves he'd prefer she not flaunt the way she did. Her formerly round face had become angular in all the right ways, and her prominent lips had turned pouty. Her beauty paired with her outgoing spirit to attract every father's worst nightmare—shallow men bent on having a good time.

Isabella ate up the attention like someone starved for affection. For that, Tim blamed himself, but he was here. He was trying. Really trying.

Besides, she'd accepted a marriage proposal from one such shallow man. So what was she doing, flashing dreamy smiles at this one?

Philip crossed his arms. "What happened at the end of the drive?"

"I think she hoped to get back to New York a few days sooner than we'd planned. When she found out I planned this stop to hear a band that won't play for a few days ..." He shrugged. He couldn't help that forest fires in and around some national parks out West had removed stops from their itinerary.

Philip peered toward the dark space beyond the bar. "Million Dollar Ransom is coming from an hour away, but if I tell them you need to hear them before Saturday, they'll be here."

"Nah." Tim glanced back to his daughter. She caught him looking and cocked a defensive eyebrow. "We need the time. She and I have unfinished business."

Amusement and leery curiosity warred on Philip's face. "Which is ...?"

"To talk her out of marrying the wrong guy at the wrong time for the wrong reasons."

Philip punctuated his slow nod with an exaggerated frown. "That's a lot of wrongs."

"Not enough to make a right." Tim would know. His marriage to Isabella's mom had lasted three months. He loved his daughter and wouldn't trade her, but all the pain he'd felt and caused in the brief marriage? Not so much. Issy could not repeat his mistakes.

Looking beyond him, Philip seemed to stifle a cringe.

Tim turned and saw that the waiter had taken a seat with

Isabella. "What's his story?" Tim growled the question through gritted teeth.

"David goes through girlfriends faster than Gannon wears out guitar strings."

As the lead singer and guitarist of Awestruck, the most successful band Tim had ever managed, Gannon Vaughn used to replace his strings every couple of weeks.

In the booth, Isabella spoke with her hands. Her fiancé was as broke as she was, so her tiny engagement ring barely caught the light, but the waiter had to notice it.

Tim stuck his hands in his pockets and stopped supervising. "Gannon's slowed down since you quit Awestruck. As far as guitar strings go, anyway. He's just as busy in every other sense. Between his family, working with younger artists, and the side projects he picks up, he's always got something going."

Philip quirked his eyebrows as if to ask if the fault in the analogy mattered.

It didn't. Even if David the Waiter would trample the engagement, Isabella wouldn't. Not when she'd spent eighty percent of this trip insisting Lars was worthy of her.

Lars. Swedes could pull off the name, but a dark-haired actor from Jersey?

"Nila's seventeen." Philip volunteered the fact about his own daughter, then paused. "That makes Isabella twenty-one?"

"Twenty-three."

Philip let out a low whistle. "We're getting old."

The statement held more truth than Tim cared to admit. Before he had to muster a response, a warm chuckle drew his attention.

"Speak for yourself." The woman who'd been in the booth with Philip approached, the younger man—her son?—shadowing her. She was even more striking up close, and no ring sparkled on her finger as she gripped her purse strap.

At her silent hint—a raised eyebrow and a tilt of the head—

Philip dove into introductions. "Gabby, I'd like you to meet Tim Bergeron. He's the guy to know if you want to break into the music industry."

She hummed a laugh. "Here to poach our star?"

Five men comprised the band Million Dollar Ransom, so she didn't mean them. Had Philip failed to mention other talent? Perhaps. He understood Tim had to be picky, and because he hadn't recommended any other acts, his suggestion of Million Dollar Ransom had piqued Tim's interest. But the last thing he wanted was to dismiss an artist this woman thought deserved a shot. "Which star?"

"Blaze Astley." The emphasis Gabby put on the name was a verbal equivalent of writing it in lights.

The younger guy who'd followed Gabby over frowned. If he was her son, was she divorced? Never married? Married but didn't wear a ring? One didn't get to their fifties without a history—Tim included. What was hers?

"Blaze sings here a few nights a week with the house band." Philip's tone held respect, but not the over-the-top enthusiasm he'd expressed for Million Dollar Ransom. "She has a strong local fan base."

"You *must* come see her. She's on tonight, right, Philip?"

"That she is."

"I'm afraid my date might not go for it." Tim hiked his thumb toward his daughter. "Although based on how our road trip is going, I'm not sure there's much Isabella *would* enjoy." At least, not if it involved Tim.

"I have daughters her age. A night out with friends could be just the thing for her." Gabby motioned to the table. "She's met David. My Charity and other young people will be here. Anson, you coming?"

Gabby's shadow shrugged. "Probably."

"There. The kids can all hang out. We can give them some space and grab a table at the back."

Locals often overestimated their favorite performers' potential, and Tim only had room for one new act. So why was he tempted to commit? Isabella would throw a fit if he worked tonight, but if he made social plans, would she be glad to have him out of her hair?

"Blaze is worth hearing." Gabby slung her purse over her shoulder and touched his arm. "You're going to love her."

Tingles raced up his arm at the contact. If a casual touch affected him so strongly, perhaps his doctor ought to run more tests. As Gabby lowered her hand, he fought to avoid rubbing the lingering tickle.

Anson's frown deepened. "The Depot wouldn't be the same without her."

Philip's expression turned smug. "I doubt anyone's going to convince her to leave, but you're welcome to try."

Tim was a professional convincer. As a band manager, he convinced temperamental artists to work with producers, labels to offer more money, venues to beef up security. Whatever it took to set his clients up for success. Convincing musicians to take a shot on their dreams? Easiest part of his job.

But again, he had to be selective. Launching a career took time and energy, and his recent brush with mortality had reminded him he had limited years to make a mark. He had to choose well.

"I've got to get going." Anson stepped toward the door. "Nice meeting you, Tim. See ya, Gabby. Philip."

Huh. If he called her by her first name, he probably wasn't her son.

Gabby's intelligent brown eyes focused up at him. Her confident personality didn't come from height. The top of her head reached Philip's shoulder and Tim's chin. "If you're not here for Blaze, Tim, what brings you to Many Oaks?"

Answers popped to mind. A health concern. His daughter. His career. He worked his knuckles against his back. Despite all those hours in the car, he and Isabella had made painfully little progress. "So many things, I don't know where to start."

"How about there?" Philip tipped his head toward Isabella's booth. The waiter had left her, and she glared daggers at Tim.

His daughter was the most important motivation for this trip, but his improved priorities hadn't healed the damage his neglect and immaturity had done during her childhood.

They might never.

But he and Isabella had already come hundreds of miles. What trouble was walking another forty feet to try connecting yet again?

"I'd better head over." He noted the empathy and encouragement in Gabby's smile. His daughter's company wasn't likely to be as kind, but Isabella was already angry over how much time and energy he devoted to his career. He couldn't further divide his attention. "Not sure about the show tonight. Sorry."

Gabby waved a hand. "If we see you, we see you. If not, I hope it means you had a breakthrough with your daughter."

"You and me both." He excused himself and tried, once again, to cross the distance between himself and his only child.

2

———————

The luster had worn off life in Many Oaks. Or so Gabby had thought until Philip introduced Tim. Excitement continued to sparkle as she watched him sit across from his daughter. Her inability to make out what he said meant she was free to speak without being overheard. "In the stories you've told about him, you never mentioned he looks like that reality TV chef who yells at everybody."

Philip snorted and assessed his former manager. "Is that good or bad?"

"As long as he doesn't have a fiery temper, good." The lines that lent his face a serious air would accent his smiles in the most endearing way. His blond hair flipped and flopped in a state of disarray she guessed was constant. Also endearing.

The poorly masked exasperation as he faced his daughter ... again, endearing. The man was trying his best, Gabby was certain, but had no idea what he was doing.

"I'm not sure I see a resemblance," Philip said.

Either way, attraction hadn't sideswiped her in how long? And now, her heart got all worked up over a visiting stranger. Perhaps the reaction made sense, given her recent longing for adventure, but she'd envisioned sating it through travel, not infatuations with friends of friends.

A crash by the bar drew Philip's attention. A waiter had dropped a stack of glasses. "Duty calls."

So much the better. She'd have to hurry if she wanted to catch her daughter during her work break. After a stop at the coffeehouse on the town square to buy a drink and a muffin for Charity, she continued to the commercial area on the other side of Many Oaks. She pulled into the lot of a large building made of cinder block and metal.

Seated at a picnic table set away from the entrance, Charity offered a wave.

Gabby collected a document scanner she'd ordered online from her back seat. She stacked the bagged muffin on top. Once confident she'd balanced the load in one hand, she lifted the latte from the holder and exited the car. She committed details about her daughter to memory as she crossed the lawn. If all went according to plan, she'd want the mental picture.

Charity had bleached her hair blonde, save for some dark roots. Gabby struggled to consider the shag haircut trendy, but Charity swore it was. The hair, paired with the boxy top and those jeans, left her daughter looking primed for a 90s-themed party—like all the other stylish twentysomethings.

Gabby was less interested in keeping up with trends, but she had happily reincorporated wide-leg, high-waisted pants into her wardrobe. With their roomy calves and thighs, they complimented her in a way skinny jeans never had—by allowing her pear-shaped body to slip into a smaller size. The fabric of said dress pants swished against her legs as she made her way to her daughter.

Charity looked toward the building entrance and sighed. Sweet and sensitive, she never should've taken the sales job, but she seemed determined to make it work. Perhaps she wanted to prove herself. Or perhaps she was afraid to risk failure by pursuing her dreams.

Before Gabby allowed herself to follow her own dreams, she needed to know her daughter was on the right track. Hence, the scanner.

Charity stood as she neared, eyeing the gifts Gabby brought. "Your birthday's coming up, not mine."

Charity had campaigned to throw her a party for her fiftieth, but Gabby had negotiated her down to a quiet dinner out. Natalie, Gabby's eldest, was flying in Thursday for the occasion. Rehashing the plan would only reignite Charity's interest in a big bash. Ignoring the statement, Gabby set the coffee and bakery bag on the table, then presented the scanner to Charity.

Her daughter read the box. "What's this about?"

"It's for your art." Even saying the words conjured mental images of the fanciful watercolors Charity had painted as a girl. More recently, with only the help of a few online tutorials, she'd produced stunning paintings. A cat studying a goldfish, a comet flashing across the night sky, a bee visiting a sunflower.

Confusion rippled across Charity's face.

"You once mentioned selling greeting cards. This is the recommended way to digitize your work so you can reproduce it or sell it online."

"I don't paint much anymore." Charity splayed her pinkies and ring fingers away from the box, as though the cardboard were burning her digits, one by one. "It was a fun way to blow off steam in college, but it wasn't a career."

"Dream a little." Gabby nudged her arm. The phrase had been Aunt Gladys's battle cry. If she and her daughters realized only a fraction of the dreams Aunt Gladys had before she passed, their lives would be wild successes. So far, only Natalie, Gabby's older daughter, was making headway toward the endeavor. At twenty-six, she already worked as a director at an up-and-coming beauty brand.

Convincing Charity to bust out of her rut would be easier if she recognized she was stuck in one. The job was only the start of it. She'd also let her faith stagnate, and her boyfriend was as much of a dead end as this company.

One problem at a time.

"Selling your work could be the perfect blend of your business skills and creativity."

Charity shook her head as she set the box on the table. "That's a sweet idea, Mom, but I already have a job. I don't know when I'd find the time to start another one."

"You'd only have to do both until you started making an income on art." With what she hoped was a winning smile, she passed Charity the coffee.

Almost as though to hide flattered disbelief, Charity lifted the cup to her lips. When she lowered it again, she glanced back at the scanner. "You can return it for your money back. If I do ever want to sell art, my phone takes crisp pictures."

"The video said the scanner captures higher resolution images than a phone. It'll give you an edge on the competition."

"You did a lot of research."

Gabby tweaked her daughter's elbow. "You have so many gifts, and it's hard to see you so stressed. I want you to know you have options."

"I do. This isn't forever. Management positions open up often enough, and then I'll be the one calling the shots."

"You'd make a great manager. But in a toxic workplace, there's only so much a great manager can do."

Charity quirked an eyebrow. "Like how a coach can only do so much with a small-town basketball team?"

Embarrassment flushed Gabby's cheeks. Ten years after losing him, reminders of her late husband usually brought gratitude. His ongoing legacy, especially in her daughters' lives and in the lives of his former athletes, had played a key role in her healing.

So the embarrassment today?

She blamed that on meeting an interesting man at The Depot. An interesting and attractive man whose very presence had gotten her to consider something she hadn't done since Judah—dipping a toe back in the dating pool. Would her daughters mind? Obviously, she was free to move on, but she was already planning other changes. Something big that Charity, especially—

"Mom?"

Gabby tugged her collar. "I have no doubt that if you put your mind to it, you can get promoted, but that doesn't mean you'll find it fulfilling. I'm hoping to add more adventure to my life, and I'd love to see you do the same."

Charity's eyes narrowed with suspicion.

"Planning to go to The Depot tonight?" Gabby's words carried high and light, like the whistle of a guilty person trying to appear innocent.

"Probably." Charity grated the three syllables against a healthy store of skepticism.

Gabby inhaled, but suddenly it seemed meddlesome to ask Charity to keep an eye out for Isabella. And Charity might ask questions that would lead to Tim.

"What's going on?"

"Oh." Gabby swiped a hand through the air as if to dismiss a joke. "Philip has some out-of-town guests visiting. One is your age. I may have suggested she could hang out with you and your friends."

"You set up a play date?" Charity's smirk said she was still suspicious, but not annoyed, at least.

"You'll keep an eye out for her? Her name's Isabella. She'll be the one with long blonde hair and—"

"And the only stranger in the place."

Not exactly, because if Isabella came, Tim would too.

Would it be awkward to spend time with Tim while Charity

was present? Or would she think nothing of it? Or be happy for her?

"You're acting weird."

This was ridiculous. Why make a federal case of attraction? She didn't even have to explain the draw to herself. She could just enjoy the chemistry.

Assuming she ever saw Tim again.

"Isabella may not come, but if she does, I'm sure she'll appreciate you."

"Okay." Charity checked the time on her phone, then slid it into her pocket. She eyed Gabby as though she wanted to press but instead collected the muffin and latte and stepped away.

Gabby lifted the scanner from the table. "Don't forget this."

"I didn't." Charity's sing-songy inflection reminded Gabby of raising teenagers.

Okay. Fine. She would deliver it another way. One that would be harder to refuse. "Have a good day. Love you."

"Love you too." Charity disappeared into the building.

Gabby eyed the box in her hand. Convincing the girl to eat her broccoli had been easier than talking her into making a life for herself that she enjoyed. Maybe she'd inherited Gabby's reluctance, if the prospect of enjoying an evening out with someone new had Gabby in such a fluster.

It's an opportunity, Aunt Gladys would say. *Run with it.*

Gabby intended to.

3

———————

"The meeting's Friday." Anson's smile held a dollop of worry.

Gabby patted the hand he rested on her table at The Depot. "You'll be fine. They respect you and want a solution as much as you do."

His nod conveyed growing confidence. "Thank you for your advice."

"Anytime." She gave his hand another squeeze to reinforce the point, though her desire to check the entry one more time trumpeted a competing message—that she was not available to give advice *any* time. For example, if Tim appeared, Gabby would rather not have an audience. Hence the reason she'd chosen a table on the periphery of the music hall.

Anson had encountered drama with some parents of students he coached. He'd sought her counsel over lunch and had stopped at her table with an update. She suspected he would've come to the same conclusion—sit everyone down and talk it out—without her involvement, but she relished being a sounding board for her late husband's protégé.

Even as a member of Judah's last basketball team, dutiful

Anson had related better to Judah than to the other Lions. Since high school, he'd become a youth pastor and a basketball coach. He'd been dating Sydney, the director of the community center, for a while now.

When he'd taken a seat next to Gabby, Sydney had remained standing. An elderly man zoomed up to propose nightly seniors' activities at the community center. Bless her heart, Sydney nodded along with kind understanding.

"That new doctor came back to small group." Implications twinkled in Anson's eyes.

That new doctor was a colleague of Gabby's. The handsome physician had won the hearts of a small town that had adored his predecessor. Not an easy feat. He'd make a great catch for someone, but Gabby's heart didn't trip at the sight of him like it had when she'd first spotted Tim. Until that moment, she'd believed romance was a thing of her past.

And maybe it still was. With Tim only passing through and her own hope of leaving Many Oaks soon herself, a lasting romance was unlikely, if not impossible.

A blond man in a navy-blue button-down passed the bar and entered the music venue. Tim. Her heartbeat kicked up. He'd changed since earlier, confirming she'd made the right decision when she'd done the same. Angel choirs had sung when she'd spotted this royal purple, flowy top in her closet tonight.

A contrast to his crisp shirt, Tim's untamed hair added to her suspicion that he'd lived an interesting life thus far. She dipped her head, hiding her amusement from Anson. Tousled hair wasn't the surest bet for judging a stranger's life. However, Gabby knew two others who'd worked in the music industry. Philip was a bona-fide former rock star. His wife was off on tour as a pop singer. The couple could tell entertaining stories for hours—and not one tale would involve sickness, bodily fluids, or death, key ingredients in the stories people in Gabby's industry told.

Tim eyed a group at the bar-height tables centered at the back. Surrounded by friends—several Lions and others—Charity and Isabella clinked glasses. Reese, Charity's boyfriend, stood nearby, absorbed in his phone. David, not waiting on tables tonight, leaned close to Tim's daughter and whispered in her ear, earning a frown from Tim.

The speakers thumped. Blaze, Philip, and the rest of the house band found their places onstage. A gust of wistful longing filled Gabby and escaped in a sigh. Their performances transformed The Depot from a small-town restaurant to a musical hotspot any big city would envy. Blaze's talent and Philip's leadership with the support band were to thank for that.

Tim seemed to tear his glare away from David and scanned the tables. Looking for her? She lifted her hand, and he started her way. Her stomach flipped. With effort, she yanked her focus back to her present company.

Anson tipped his head with interest and ... concern? Was her crush obvious?

She needed a distraction pronto.

Sydney remained trapped in conversation with the older gentleman. "We have a committee for senior's activities," the younger woman said. "I'm sure there's space for you, and you have all these ideas—"

Henry launched into excuses to avoid the commitment.

Gabby pointed Anson toward his girlfriend and lowered her voice to a murmur. "If that isn't your opportunity to rescue a damsel in distress, I don't know what is."

He sized up Sydney's company and hid his reply behind a loose fist. "She can handle herself. Trust me."

"I'm sure she can, but the occasional rescue keeps the

romance alive." How many times had she been grateful for Judah's rescue?

She'd never dreamed of becoming a mom before meeting him. Afterward, a matching desire for children took root. Still, she'd never aspired to stay at home. During her first pregnancy, she'd mentioned her plan to continue nursing to a group of other moms.

Their judgmental disapproval had her teetering on the verge of tears when Judah tucked her under his arm and whisked her away. Once he'd gotten her alone, he'd listened as she repeated their arguments for giving up her career, then offered counterpoints that left her feeling confident and cherished as both her career and their small family grew.

She'd still wished they could travel more, but for the most part, the life they'd built together fulfilled her. Only recently had the wind begun to change again, as though God was leading her back to aspirations she'd long since written off.

Tim set his glass next to hers and pulled out a chair.

Anson joined Sydney. He didn't take her hand. Didn't even touch her back. The lack of contact seemed incongruent with their year-long relationship. Did those two *have* a romance to keep alive? In a moment, he'd extricated her from the conversation, and the pair joined up with their friends.

Gabby turned her attention and found Tim's piercing blue eyes on her. Puffs of confetti exploded in her midsection. She waited just long enough to calm her voice. "Your date ditched you already?"

He nodded once. "Your plan worked. Although, I suspect it's more Casanova than your daughter she's interested in connecting with."

"David?" He maintained his place next to Isabella, but he wasn't acting any more romantically inclined than Anson with Sydney. He did have a rather long list of exes, however. "He's a decorated war vet, if that helps. One of these days, someone special is going to catch his eye, and he'll settle down."

"Not reassuring. Isabella's supposedly engaged to a guy she swears is a winner."

Gabby laughed. "Supposedly? Which part is in doubt?"

"There's a ring, so I believe they're engaged."

That left the quality of the man up for debate. By the bar, Charity's boyfriend had looped an arm around her waist.

"I suppose I'm lucky Charity's not serious about the guy she's seeing. Reese pays his phone more attention than her, and she almost never mentions him. When she does, she doesn't light up. Honestly, I don't know why they're together."

"Not enough prospects in Many Oaks?" Tim quipped.

There hadn't been until Tim showed up, not for Gabby anyway. A blush tingled across her cheeks. "There are a few her age, but I suppose most of the boys in that group—David included—had my late husband as their high school basketball coach. Out of respect for him, they treat my daughters like their sisters. That may be why Natalie moved away—to find boys who didn't think of her as Coach's daughter."

Tim studied her. Oh, she'd gone and done it—mentioned her late husband. Should she explain? The moment broke as Tim's attention returned to his daughter.

"How long are you here for?" A time frame would help her decide how personal to get.

"We leave Sunday morning." He continued to observe Isabella and David, obviously more concerned about them than about Judah.

"Less than a week." Gabby's voice lifted. With Tim just passing through, the stakes were low for both her heart and his daughter's. "How much trouble can she get in?"

Tim grunted. "Plenty. Split-second decisions change lives." He spared Gabby an apologetic smile. "Hazard of my job. I watch it happen all the time."

"Well." She tucked her fingers under her thighs. If Isabella and David's decisions this week could change the courses of their lives, her own decisions and interactions held the same power. This might not be the harmless crush she'd thought. Even so, Tim might benefit from rosier glasses. "I'm sure it'll all work out in the end."

Blaze took the mic from its stand, and Tim's focus shifted to the stage.

Gabby didn't bother to stifle her smile of giddy anticipation. The singer's voice might just restore his optimism. And through Tim, Blaze could break out. Since Gabby couldn't pursue her own dreams quite yet, she'd love to watch someone else achieve theirs.

TIM REGULARLY DECLINED "OPPORTUNITIES," but he didn't want to shoot down Gabby. He'd have to, of course. He only had one slot. The girl on stage was beautiful, but being a star required an X-factor few possessed. Odds were, Blaze didn't have it. Would Gabby understand? Or would she make this awkward?

Probably the latter, given how the trip was going. This afternoon they'd ventured an hour from Many Oaks to a state park. In theory they could've talked while they hiked, except he'd been occupied trying to keep up with Isabella's boundless energy. He'd been taking better care of himself lately, but the brisk pace and ninety-degree heat had done him in. By the time they returned to the car, he was a sweaty mess. When Isabella noticed, she'd somehow twisted his intentions, accusing him of thinking she was a "terrible person" who wouldn't slow down for her own father.

Assuring her it'd been his own pride and not a low opinion of her that had kept him from complaining hadn't softened her.

They'd cleaned up at the rental, dined in tense silence, and been only too happy to part ways afterward.

"Welcome to The Depot." At Blaze's sultry voice, some turned their attention to the stage. Others continued their conversations. "I'm Blaze, and this is The Signalmen." She indicated the band backing her up as the music started.

Familiar music.

Blaze wrapped her hand around the microphone and belted out the opening lyrics. "You asked, and I always answered, a slave to your beck and call."

This was a classic Awestruck song called "Not Your Hero."

Philip shot Tim a grin from stage, but the quick look couldn't explain whether covering one of Awestruck's hits had been the plan all along or if they'd made a last-minute adjustment for Tim. The choice invited a direct comparison to Gannon Vaughn's powerhouse voice. The bold move paid off. Blaze packed a few punches of her own, and her energetic performance commanded the room's attention.

Gabby tweaked an eyebrow as though to ask, *Good, right?*

Tim nodded once. But good enough for his last spot? He'd need to hear more than a cover to decide.

He refocused on the woman next to him. Her deep purple top skimmed her figure and complimented the brown of her eyes, but earlier, she'd worn a crisp white shirt with an office vibe. He spoke over the thudding music. "What do you do, Gabby?"

"I'm a nurse practitioner."

A healthcare worker? All the gibberish he'd been learning would make perfect sense to her, but if he wasn't interested in 99.9 percent of the bands people pitched when they heard he worked in music, she didn't want to hear about an acquaintance's health issues. He propped an elbow on the table and angled closer.

Curiosity in her eyes, she tipped her head to listen.

"Is now when most people lower their voice and ask awkward health questions?"

Grinning, she sat back in her chair. "More often than I'd like. But that's a small price to pay for a rewarding job. I believe God called me to it."

"You're a Christian?"

"Since kindergarten. You?"

"Yes, but only for the last few years." He'd chosen his career all on his own. Or had his passion for music been a gift from a God he hadn't yet known? Possibly. Working with Awestruck, a secular rock band made up of believers, had eventually led him to Christ. "How long have you been in nursing?"

"Since college, but I didn't get my master's and become a nurse practitioner until the girls were in school. How about you? How does one become a music manager?"

"One relationship at a time. I interned for a label, got to know Lee Ballard, kind of an icon in the business. He was ..." Tim hesitated. He'd come to have had a lot in common with Lee. Not that he'd call himself an icon, but he faced similar options—either refrain from taking on too many acts or hire someone to work under him. "He wanted to expand his roster beyond what he could manage himself, so he brought me on as an associate. After a few years, I went out on my own."

"And what do managers do?"

"Guide artists to doors and make sure those doors are open."

Most people accepted the elusive answer and moved on. Gabby's eyes narrowed as though trying to understand and failing. Her authentic interest warmed him.

"I promote my artists to everybody who can help build their careers. I also advise on business decisions, negotiate contracts, help with the creative process, and get involved with marketing and tours. About the only thing I *don't* do is pick up an instrument or start singing."

"Would we want you to?" A sly smile accompanied the question.

"We would not."

Gabby chuckled. "Then what drew you into the music industry in the first place?"

"My parents always had the radio on. After their divorce, I lived with my mom, but Dad and I traded mixtapes once or twice a year—my birthday and, sometimes, Christmas. He told me I had good taste."

"And when that's the only contact a boy has with his dad, the compliment sticks."

"That it does." Tim had resented his dad's disinterest, but the compliment had inspired confidence in his own taste in music.

She peered toward their daughters. "It's amazing the effect absent people have. The littlest things from them have the biggest impact."

He suspected she was thinking of her late husband, but the statement applied to his own situation as well. "For better or worse."

Gabby's cocked eyebrow asked him to explain.

If he opened up, she might too. "I was absent for Isabella's childhood. She was a teenager when I came to Christ. Even then, I didn't step up the way I wish I had. Now she's bent on repeating my mistakes."

"How so?"

"She's rushing into marriage. Her mom and I ..." He hesitated, but his failed marriage was part of his story. "We were married three months. Again, this was before Christ. We were terrible to each other. I want to stop Issy from getting on that rollercoaster."

Gabby nodded, compassion in her expression. "Our jobs would be much easier if we could make their choices for them."

Tim grunted.

"So you mentioned this is a road trip. From where to where?"

"My place to hers. We started in LA, and she lives in New York City."

"Oh, wow. That's fantastic." Gabby's enthusiasm made his disappointment stand out all the more.

"I wish. We've been having problems from the start. There are wildfires in and around some of the national parks out West, so we took a few stops out of our itinerary. Hence our arrival on Monday for a show that's not happening until Saturday night. Then there's the bigger issue that this trip was supposed to give us quality father-daughter time, and you can see how that's going." He lifted a hand to where Isabella followed David onto the dance floor. They were part of a larger group, and the music was fast, not romantic.

Still. What was she thinking? If this was how she protected a relationship that she swore was important to her, her marriage would last no longer than his had—if she made it down the aisle at all. While he was in favor of breaking the engagement, there was a way to do things. Namely, give the ring back *before* getting involved with someone new. Even better, stay single unless a worthy suitor came along—one who, for example—knew better than to flirt with a woman with a ring on her finger.

He pulled his attention back to his companion. "How long have you lived in Many Oaks?"

"Since before the girls were born—I have two daughters. Charity lives in town. Natalie is up in the Twin Cities. Judah and I married in college. When he graduated, he cast a wide net, applying all over the country to teaching jobs that would also allow him to coach basketball. When the offer from Many Oaks came, we noticed the mascot was a lion. We joked that Judah's Lions had a certain ring to it."

"Biblical, almost."

"Exactly. Silly, but the idea took root. We talked about only staying a few years, but time got away from us. I think Judah liked it here more than he expected to."

"You didn't?"

"I felt welcomed and safe here, but I ..." Her hesitation seemed packed with meaning, but then she threw him off with a smile. "How many states have you been to? This road trip alone must've crossed off quite a few."

Except that he'd been to them all already. He hadn't tracked, but Awestruck's tour manager had, checking each state off until the band had performed in each one. Between shows he'd attended and other travel, he'd visited all fifty. He sensed that answer would discourage Gabby, so he side-stepped it. "I travel with my bands quite a bit."

"And how many countries have you seen?"

He'd stopped counting a long time before. "A few."

Gabby's chin dipped with what looked like disappointment.

"How about you? Travel much?" Given her reaction, he suspected she hadn't, but if she cared so much, why hadn't she made it a priority?

"Twelve states, three countries."

"That's a decent start." Better than he'd expected, based on her apparent envy.

Gabby tipped her head side-to-side. "One of my aunts was a stewardess. She visited every state and continent—including Antarctica, thanks to a cruise she took in retirement—and something like fifty countries before she died a few years ago. I grew up wanting to be like her—such a vivacious world traveler. But God had other plans. My parents insisted I get a college degree as a fallback plan in case being a flight attendant didn't work out."

"You ended up marrying in college."

She nodded. "Judah and I met at the university. Falling in love changed everything."

"Family life is its own adventure." Since he'd made such a mess of being a father, he respected parents who put their kids first. "It's not too late to fill in the gaps. Get out there more."

She leaned in. "Between you and me, I do have an idea." Her voice carried just loud enough for him to discern a lift of excitement.

This sounded like a secret. Did she trust him already? His heartbeat responded to the possibility with alarming enthusiasm. "Which is?"

She bit her lip as though to keep her plans from bursting out. He could've booed as she settled back in her chair, sadness tempering her excitement. "I have some unfinished business to resolve before getting carried away. My daughter isn't in the best place."

"Mine isn't either, but that doesn't have to dictate our whole lives." Or did it? Tim could manage a band, but a daughter?

Gabby changed the subject, and he let her. How would he encourage a near stranger when he had so little of his own life together?

4

———————

Tim had come to hear a band, yet he hadn't expected talent of the caliber Blaze displayed with each lyric she belted out. At the bar, he ordered fresh sodas for himself and Gabby. While he waited for the bartender to fill the order, he turned toward the stage. The Signalmen had performed mostly covers, but they now offered their fourth original of the night.

Blaze's voice soared, hands midair, fingers spread as though to release even more post-teen pop angst. In such rich, clean tones, she could captivate an audience by singing the alphabet, let alone such emotional songs. By joining forces—her voice, looks, and stage presence combined with his business sense and connections—they could make a mint.

No wonder she'd packed the place, even on a Monday night, and Anson, Gabby's younger friend, hadn't wanted to think about her leaving. Yet artists made most of their money from touring. To attract a label, she might first have to build a broader fan base by touring.

Was Philip correct? Would she refuse to leave Many Oaks?

"You're into Charity's mom?" Isabella perched on the barstool beside him.

He leaned an elbow on the bar top, trying to get his balance as he pulled himself from Blaze's potential.

Standing directly behind Isabella, Charity crossed her arms, a knowing smile on her lips, as though she'd caught him gazing at Gabby rather than the performance. That the girls watched him as closely as he'd watched Isabella and David shouldn't surprise him.

"Good," Isabella said. "Charity needs your help."

"With what?" He glanced at Charity, but she watched Isabella.

"Distracting her," his daughter said. "Her mom's birthday is Saturday. They're planning a huge surprise bash here Friday night because of the Million Dollar Ransom show Saturday." She pursed her lips as though to guilt trip him for his interest in the band. "It'd be helpful if you'd keep her busy so she doesn't catch on. Just until Friday night, since we're going to be around anyway." She gave a pointed look. Another guilt trip, this one for keeping her from Lars.

He did owe her. Not for detaining her, but for keeping secrets so she'd agree to this trip at all.

The bartender set the sodas he'd ordered on the bar. Tim passed him cash but didn't move to take the drinks. "How do you suggest I do that? It's only Monday."

"Well, we won't be working on the party the *whole* time." Isabella looked to Charity.

"Tomorrow night and Friday at lunch are the important ones."

Isabella nodded as if that decided something. She returned her focus to Tim. "Take her on a few dates."

"I'm not leading her on." The words tasted bitter, since he was, in a different way, leading Isabella on.

"You don't like her?"

"I do, but—"

"Ever heard of a whirlwind romance?" Charity quipped.

"I don't think those can be manufactured."

"She likes you." Arms still threaded together, Charity lifted a finger toward the table where Gabby waited. "We bought that top together ages ago, but she hasn't worn it. She's trying to impress you."

Extra effort hadn't been necessary. But at the suggestion that she'd taken extra care, glowing pressure built in his chest. These reactions took some getting used to.

Isabella made shooing motions. "Go ask her out."

Tim hadn't always been one to deny himself a good time, but he'd matured these last few years. Or so he hoped. He stood his ground. "This won't work the way you think it will."

Charity tapped her fingers against her arm. "I know her. It'll be fine. It's just two dates."

Across the room, Gabby met his gaze and smiled before refocusing on the stage. She was intelligent, hardworking, and interesting to talk to. He wouldn't mind a shot at learning more about those plans of hers.

Yet, he couldn't undermine his relationship with his daughter. "This will tie up more of my schedule. Is that what you want?"

"What I want matters?"

Only Isabella could flood him with such a mix of love and frustration. He pulled out a barstool and sat. "Sorry, then. Can't help."

"Okay, we get it." Charity nudged the sodas closer. "You care about your daughter."

He doubted either of the girls did get it, but both seemed to consider the matter closed because they started toward their friends.

A light touch to Isabella's elbow stopped her. She turned back to him, wariness in her expression.

"What you want hasn't always mattered the way it should've, but I've changed."

Emotions paraded, one after the other, across her face. Uncertainty, skepticism, and maybe, if he wasn't letting his own hopes read into things, gratitude. "You don't have anything to prove, Dad. We're stuck here for days. If we spend all that time together, we both know we'll be at each other's throats. This is best. Go, have fun."

Gabby's foot pumped as she resisted intruding on the trio at the bar. She so wanted to brag on Charity and meet Isabella. If Gabby brought up Charity's work troubles, Tim, who'd succeeded in business, would have good advice for her.

But Charity wouldn't appreciate her praise or meddling, and if Tim wished to introduce Gabby to Isabella, he'd do so. As passing acquaintances, introductions served little purpose.

He returned to the table. "Our daughters seem to have hit it off."

She bumped his arm, and her heart thumped at the contact. "I told you. A night with friends was just the thing."

"One night with friends has led to days' worth of plans with friends." He cringed, though he didn't appear disappointed. "It seems I'll have some time to kill." A question lurked in his eyes.

Or was it an invitation?

Did he *like* her?

Her high school self was back to haunt her. Teenage memories of Aunt Gladys also surfaced. *Of course he likes you. What's not to like?*

She'd been single so long, she couldn't say. Instead of acting on assumptions, she opted to tease. "Is that any way to live? Just killing time? Wasting it?"

His purposeful eye contact froze her smile in place, and she held her breath as he replied. "Time spent in good company isn't wasted."

A flattered laugh slipped from her lips.

"How about dinner and a movie?"

"That sounds like a date." Fearing rejection, she dropped her gaze, but it bounced right back up again. Curiosity sure was a buoyant thing.

Tim gave a warm smile. "I should hope so."

"Tomorrow?" Gabby asked. The suddenness prompted another laugh. She might not be able to act on her larger plan for adventure, but if nothing else, a date or two would serve as a refreshing detour from her rut. "Many Oaks has a wonderful farm-to-table Italian restaurant, but the closest thing we have to a movie theater is when the community center puts up its projector for outdoor showings."

Tim frowned thoughtfully, then nodded once. "Let's plan for dinner and see where the night takes us."

Far be it from her to reject an invitation to an adventure. "I'm in."

5

———

The butterflies in Gabby's stomach behaved more like bunny rabbits. Playful, but skittish. She hadn't been on a date in ten years. She hadn't been on a *first* date in about thirty. She hadn't been the *driver* on a first date in ever. However, this was her home turf, and she'd volunteered to drive herself and Tim to Meliore's Ristorante Italiano.

After her last patient and the associated paperwork, she touched up her eyeliner and lipstick in the clinic bathroom, then texted Tim as she left the building. *On my way.*

Moments later, the phone buzzed in her hand, and one of the bunnies did a backflip. *Ready*, he'd written.

She was excited, but was she ready? The word implied confidence in the ability to impress she couldn't claim, but her nerves weren't enough to keep her from trying. She was the embodiment of *ready or not, here I come.*

She slung her purse into the back seat. It thumped into the scanner she still hadn't gotten to Charity. The bag toppled, but none of its contents spilled, as if to promise the night would go smoothly. She got behind the wheel to go pick up her date.

Her date!

Six minutes later, she navigated the last turn. Who knew Many Oaks attracted enough visitors to have vacation rentals? The driveway was set off to the side, and a walk extended from the front door, across the small front yard to the curb, so she pulled up there. The dated exterior of the home appeared well-maintained. Would she see the interior at some point? One of the bunnies jumped and twisted.

Tim paused to lock up and started for her car. He wore another dark button-down with jeans and leather shoes. Warm spice floated on the air as he closed himself in the passenger seat. "I solved the movie problem."

"You built a theater today?" she teased.

"In a manner of speaking."

She kept her foot on the brake pedal to keep them at the curb. She was nervous enough. Simultaneously dealing with first-date giddiness, driving, and a puzzle would not bode well. "You talked the community center into an impromptu outdoor movie night?"

"No. There's a chance of rain." He spoke as though commandeering the community center's outdoor set-up for a date had been a serious consideration.

"Did you go to a lot of trouble?"

He clicked his seatbelt and motioned for her to drive. "A little trouble pays dividends."

Judah had lived by a set of similar sayings. Those pithy statements still peppered the conversations Gabby had with her daughters and the Lions, either slipping out of her mouth or one of theirs. A little part of a larger legacy.

Bittersweetness curled through her like steam off dandelion tea. She checked over her shoulder and pulled into the lane. She liked Tim and didn't want to think about having only memories of him to keep her company. Of course, she shouldn't be thinking that way. She hardly knew the man. She cleared her throat and grabbed the first new subject she thought of—the scanner in the back seat. "If it's all right, I'd like to swing by my daughter's apartment to drop something off."

When Tim hesitated, she second-guessed herself. Perhaps it'd been an odd request.

She rubbed her arm where the fluttery sleeve of her green satin blouse tickled her. "It's about two blocks out of the way, and I'll leave it on her porch, so we'll make our reservation. Or I can do it another time."

"I think it'll be all right. Go for it."

He *thought* it would be all right? She glanced over.

His smile almost looked guilty.

Tension stiffened her obliques. Something seemed weird here. Gabby almost retracted the suggestion, but changing her mind would make it worse, right? So, she navigated through Many Oaks and steered onto another quiet side street.

The two-story houses in Charity's neighborhood stood close together on small lots. Aside from the occasional over-grown shrub or lawn, most of the properties showed the care and attention of their owners. Parked cars by Charity's narrowed the street to one lane. She waited while another vehicle passed through before driving the congested stretch. "Someone's having a party."

Tim didn't reply. Gabby had enough to worry about anyway. She refused to hit a parked vehicle. Or a child could run into the street. But her careful surveillance registered movement in only one front yard: Charity's.

A pickup truck had parked in the mouth of her driveway. Cameron Weldon, a Lion, stood in the bed, passing boxes to former teammate Nolan Thorpe, who stacked them to be carried inside. A couch sat in the front lawn, also loaded with boxes and a couple of stuffed-full laundry baskets. A woman lifted one basket and carried it toward the duplex.

"Someone must be moving in upstairs." Hopefully Charity's new neighbor would be one of the Lions. A single one who had his life together, like Nolan. The proximity might convince her daughter life would be better with a higher-caliber boyfriend.

Gabby wedged her car into the first open spot two doors down. "I'll be right back." She gathered the scanner from the back seat and started toward the activity, but before she'd gone two steps, Tim joined her.

"Maybe this isn't a good time." The quickness of his words belied the calmness suggested by the low timbre of his voice. "Someone might swipe it."

None of the Lions would, but the woman she'd spotted might have no reason to respect Coach Judah and his family. The scanner had set her back a couple of hundred dollars. She turned the slim box in her hands. "I'll put it inside the screen door."

The plan would take patience. The woman with the laundry basket stood at the base of the stairs, watching the porch as though waiting for something. A blonde with fair skin and eyes like Tim's ... this was Isabella. She must've become fast friends with someone to help them move one day after arriving in town.

A man's voice sounded from the porch, only he wasn't exiting the upper unit. Instead, he backed out of the lower unit, Charity's apartment, hands hooked under a couch. Reese?

He turned his head to spot the steps, still walking backwards. It *was* Reese moving out Charity's saggy old couch with David's help. Charity followed them down the stairs and onto the front yard, arms full of cushions. Meanwhile, Isabella zipped into the apartment with the laundry basket. Cameron thundered in after her, a box in his arms.

Gabby shifted the scanner to one hand and braced it against her side as she stepped from the sidewalk onto the lawn. Since when did her daughter keep secrets about major developments like this? "What's going on?"

Charity whirled, face flushed and eyes wide. "Mom. What are you doing here?"

"I asked first." The words sounded like something a child would punctuate with a stomp. Gabby wished for a more mature response. What would Judah say? No answers materialized.

Twenty feet beyond her daughter, Reese and David hefted the couch into the back of the truck. After a furtive glance at Gabby, Reese said something about straps and went to the cab of the vehicle.

Charity shot a look at Tim. "I thought you two had a date."

"I thought you two had other plans." Accusation carried on Tim's tone, and displeased lines bracketed his mouth.

Light steps tapped down the stairs, and Isabella joined their cluster. Her hair was up in a sloppy bun. As she rested her hands on her hips, her chest rose and fell with heavy breaths, as though she'd made several trips in and out. "I hope you didn't come *here* for dinner."

Her light tone undermined Gabby's suspicions. Was she reading too much into this?

The others went about their business. Reese returned with a jumble of nylon ratchet straps. He kept his back to Gabby as he unknotted the mess.

Nolan carried a box inside the apartment.

"So?" Gabby prompted.

"Might as well get it over with." Isabella straightened her shoulders and lifted her chin, a mimed suggestion that Charity ought to stand up for herself.

Charity cast her newfound friend a leery glance, then sighed. Her eye contact with Gabby was fleeting, her posture more tired than empowered. "Reese is moving in."

"What?" The word thundered out of Gabby's mouth.

In the driveway, Reese dropped the straps.

David hopped from the bed of the truck to help him. Still, Reese didn't come take responsibility for what had to have been a joint decision.

Coward.

Charity crossed her arms and shifted. "We've been dating for eight months."

"Not seriously." Their form of "dating" involved hanging out at The Depot and binging television. When Gabby asked about more serious aspects of the relationship, Charity dismissed the importance. How could such a relationship be anything but casual?

Charity averted her gaze with a slow, annoyed blink.

"I thought you two weren't serious. He ..." was standing too close for Gabby to enumerate his flaws. Thankfully, Cameron and Nolan had stayed inside, away from her hissing whisper, but Isabella, David, Reese, Charity, and Tim remained in earshot in the front yard.

"You didn't *want* us to be serious. Just like you don't want me to be serious about my job or quitting church or staying in Many Oaks. But I am, Mom." Charity's voice shook. Adding more force seemed to shore it up. "I'm serious, and for once, I wish you'd be happy for me so I didn't have to tiptoe around you and hide things."

Gabby's mouth opened, but nothing—not air, not words, and certainly not the black and red emotions exploding in her chest cavity—came out. A line of pain flared across her ankle as the scanner toppled to the grass. She'd dropped it.

Her campaign to inspire Charity was supposed to be loving. Caring. Motherly. Not overbearing. Yet her daughter panted with anger even as tears lined her eyes.

Had Gabby been so far off that she deserved this public diatribe?

She checked her words.

As far as diatribes went, she'd seen worse. If Charity had bottled up resentment, at least she'd spilled it so they could begin clean-up.

Tim's hand closed around hers. She'd reached out for support without even noticing. She was too overwhelmed for a rational conversation with her daughter. Although, considering she'd apparently been racking up offenses for months, she might not do much better in her right mind.

She closed her mouth. Swallowed. Drew just enough strength from Tim's steady hold on her to address Charity. "I'd like to hear more about what you need from our relationship, but I'm going to need a few days."

Which meant her birthday dinner wouldn't be the time to tell the girls about her plans. She wouldn't have the assurances she needed about Charity's future to feel comfortable with pursuing something new. They might not even manage to eat together.

Charity blinked watery eyes and shot an uncertain glance at Reese, who continued to avoid looking in their direction. Her mouth worked like she might issue an apology. Gabby couldn't allow her to revert to maintaining false peace by stuffing down resentment. They needed open communication, the kind that wouldn't happen here and now.

Gabby scooped up the scanner. She'd return it lest it become a memorial to this falling out. She met Tim's eyes. "Let's not miss our reservation."

Tim could've glanced at the girls again. Could've shied away from the drama or managed the situation. Instead, he held Gabby's gaze a moment, then escorted her to the vehicle.

When they neared it, he held out his hand, and she gave up the keys. He got her door, closed her in the passenger seat, and wordlessly got behind the wheel.

He must've envisioned a more peaceful evening when he'd

suggested a date, yet instead of running away, he anticipated her needs. She didn't know what was true between herself and Charity anymore or what might come next, but she knew one thing. She was grateful Tim had come to town.

6

———

im had talked a lot of people into a lot of things—contracts, tours, appearances, songs, partnerships—but he prided himself on being a straight shooter. A little blunt sometimes, maybe, but whatever reasoning he offered, it was the truth.

People he worked with didn't operate by the same code, so he got everything in writing and did his homework. He researched companies, combed through contracts, and hired lawyers to identify potential problems. He didn't wait for his artists to keep him apprised of life events that could impact their career.

In retrospect, he should've been suspicious when Isabella claimed she wanted to spend the evening planning a birthday party for an acquaintance's mother. Yet he'd trusted her. He would've confronted her lie on the spot if the situation hadn't come so close to bowling Gabby right over.

Guilt bucked him off his high horse. He'd used a sizeable omission to ensure Isabella didn't back out of this trip.

In the passenger seat, Gabby worked on her phone. The screen in the dash flashed as it displayed a map with a blue line to follow to Meliore's. As an automated voice over the speakers directed him to turn right in a quarter mile, her phone clattered into a cupholder in the center console. She leaned back in her seat, eyes closed and hands clamped between her knees.

"For the record, your restraint is admirable." If he weren't driving, he'd be chewing out Isabella via text.

"That wasn't restraint. It was pure survival instinct."

"Your survival instincts are very different from mine." He took the turn onto a broader street with more traffic. "I'm more of a fight to the death kind of guy."

"That wasn't the hill to die on. I never meant for her to feel like I wasn't taking her seriously. But, wow. Living with her boyfriend ..."

Isabella's choice to live with Lars had disappointed but not surprised him. Isabella had been a teenager when Tim adopted Christianity, but Isabella remained an unbeliever. Gabby and Judah seemed to have taught their girls about Jesus from a young age, though. Given Gabby's reaction to the move-in, she must not have realized how far her daughter had strayed.

"She sprung a lot on you." His phone buzzed with a text that would have to wait until they reached the restaurant.

"I knew we saw things differently. I just didn't know I'd offended her so badly—or misunderstood her and Reese. The boy hardly looks up from his phone."

"Most in their age group don't."

"Anson's almost never on his. He's just a couple years older."

Anson. The clean-cut one. His choice to lunch with Gabby and Philip, both of whom were older than himself, suggested a preference for more settled, mature company. Meanwhile, Charity reminded him more of Isabella—edgy and impulsive. "You want her to be with Anson?"

Gabby frowned. "The point is, she could do better than Reese. And she shouldn't be moving in with anyone. I didn't realize they were physical."

GPS interrupted again, and Tim glanced at the screen to verify before changing lanes. "Because you didn't realize how she felt about him or about church."

She shrugged miserably. "She quit attending in college but wouldn't get into it with me. I assumed it was more about not wanting to give up part of her weekend than about any real change in beliefs. I didn't know she'd live such a different lifestyle. Or that I'd be the enemy for suggesting the world has more to offer than what she'll find in Many Oaks."

"You want her to move away?"

"She can't know she likes living here best without trying other places too. I don't want her boxed in."

"Like you've been?"

The silence from the passenger seat might as well have been a blaring horn, warning him he'd made a wrong turn in the conversation.

His chest tightened, but he stifled the urge to clear his throat. "I'm sure the Many Oaks thing was just a tacked-on defense."

"Even so ..."

Tim caught a flash of swirling letters on a sign. The calligraphy was too hard to decode in the split second before they passed, but GPS announced they'd reached their destination. With the parking spaces on the street full, he turned into the narrow lot. "Kids can be dramatic."

He angled the vehicle into a stall, nosing the car up to the brick building. Gabby still hadn't replied. He wanted to spend the evening together, but perhaps Charity had changed things too much for Gabby to enjoy herself.

His phone buzzed with a reminder of the text. He shifted to free the device and read Isabella's note in a glance. *They're planning a surprise party for Gabby on Friday. Don't blow it.*

If she wanted promises, she shouldn't have deceived him. Unless Charity had deceived her too? No, if that were the case, she would've led with it to deflect his frustration. He stuffed the phone away again.

The suggestion of a rain check hovered in his throat when Gabby sighed. "Maybe I was pushy about her career—I've been trying to talk her into starting an art business—but I hardly said anything about the other stuff. I mean, I did share Bible verses with her when one reminded me of her, but they were encouraging ones."

In multiple failed attempts to read through the Bible in a year, Tim had read the first few books of the Bible more times than any others. Gabby likely highlighted verses about grace and restoration instead of Old Testament laws, but he couldn't help himself. "People caught in adultery will be taken outside the camp and stoned?"

"Goodness, no." She snorted at the made-up verse and shot him a grateful look. "Besides, adultery suggests at least one of the parties is married. She hasn't gone that far."

"How's that for a silver lining?"

She sighed again. "I wish I'd listened better."

"She probably didn't tell you everything—not because of your listening skills, but because of her guilty conscience."

Gabby gave an unenthusiastic half-smile, then scanned their surroundings. "I'm not very good company, am I?"

"On the contrary. There's no one I'd rather spend the evening with—maybe because Isabella and I have been on eggshells, and misery loves company."

Wry humor lifted the corner of her mouth.

Tim continued. "Not that I want you miserable too. I did plan something I think you'll enjoy, but if you aren't up for this, I understand."

She turned her face toward the awning-covered entrance. Her hair, tucked behind her ear, revealed the faint lines of happier times fanning her temple. Even in profile, the angles of her browbone and cheek spoke of poise. Her dainty gold earring glinted as she glanced his way. "How much trouble did you go to?"

He and Isabella had spent the whole day arranging for his after-dinner plans. In part, the quality time with her helped justify the effort and the price tag—way too hefty of one for a first date. But if he didn't also get to enjoy the date, was the undertaking worth the effort? It'd have to be, because he wouldn't guilt Gabby into it.

He shook his head, refusing an answer.

"I like the idea of dinner, but I would be distracted."

"Maybe for stretches, but you'll enjoy yourself too."

Her gaze out the windshield seemed glassy and unfocused. "People are going to stare."

"Why? Does news of a little tiff travel like that here?"

"No." She cringed. "I mean, maybe, but I ... haven't been on a date in a while. People notice such things in a small town. I should've warned you."

"I'm used to famous company. They can stare all they want. They can even take pictures and ask for autographs, and I won't miss a beat."

She bit her bottom lip and aimed shining eyes at him. As the humor ebbed, she tilted her head, hair slipping and exposing a little triangle of skin by her neckline. "Oh, the ways to become famous in Many Oaks."

Yet another hint about her dissatisfaction with her town. "You don't seem to like it here."

The corner of her mouth turned down. "I never envisioned staying so long. At first, I wanted to follow my aunt's footsteps by being a flight attendant, but when Judah came along, I was okay with altering the plan. But even with him, I'd hoped we'd move around more. We agreed to only stay in Many Oaks a couple of years."

"What happened?"

"The people. They're like family. When we moved in, they

showed up with casseroles. So many casseroles." A little laugh slipped out. "Same when the girls were born. They overpaid for everything at Lions fundraisers and attended games, including those out of town. We always had plans with people from church. A few years into it, Judah was making real progress with the team, and I was busy with the girls and work. Adventure got sidelined." She fiddled with a ring she wore on her right hand. "When Judah died, well, you've never seen a town pull together like that." She had a thoughtful gleam in her eye, but her tone remained even.

"More casseroles?" Teasing was a risk.

It paid off as Gabby smiled before answering. "That and a string of prayer meetings for us and for the kids affected by the accident." She glanced at him and then away. "A semi hit the bus bringing them home from a game."

"Brutal. I'm sorry." He'd been in a car accident himself not long ago. It'd been bad enough, even without fatalities.

"It's a miracle no other lives were lost." Her chest rose with a deep breath. "In the aftermath, everyone around here banded together on our behalf. They helped with funeral arrangements. The uninjured Lions set up a schedule to mow the lawn. A former student of Judah's wouldn't hear of us paying for car repairs for a good three years. And more." Her voice thickened, and she blinked rapidly as she fell quiet.

"You were going through a lot. I'm glad people did what they could."

"I appreciate them." Gabby heaved a deep breath, eyes roving as though members of the community and not a brick wall stood in front of the vehicle. "Judah died about ten years ago, though. One of these days, I've got to stop getting emotional about what people did for us."

"When people help during tough times, the gratitude doesn't have an expiration date."

She fidgeted with an earring. "Which could explain why

I've been so hesitant to leave Many Oaks. They've been my support system. But lately, with the girls grown, I can't stop thinking about how I wanted to move around more. A travel nurse position would allow me to relocate every few months. I was considering telling my daughters I'm going for it when we had dinner together on Friday, but that's out of the question now."

"Telling them on Friday? Or going at all?"

"Both."

"Why?"

"Charity." Despair wobbled in her voice. "I can't leave when she's so lost."

Gabby wasn't responsible for Charity's choices, but then, who was he to say what good parents did or didn't do?

Rather than offer his useless advice, he brought the conversation back around. "I'm sorry about everything. Like I said, I understand if you want to call tonight off, but, hey, if you're after adventure, start small. Follow through on the date. Let people gawk. You've gotta do something with the night, right?"

Amusement crept into her features, deepening the lines beside her eyes. "Just wasting time, huh?"

She seemed to expect him to repeat what he'd said earlier about time in good company not being a waste. Instead, he took the keys from the ignition and opened his door. "I highly doubt you'll consider what I have planned a waste."

7

———

*A*fter a companionable dinner, Gabby let Tim drive her to the movie he'd promised. Or at least, that was where he said he was taking her. So why did he turn into The Depot's lot?

"Do you know how many online guides there are about the best date-night movie?" With the car parked, he handed the keys over.

Gabby chuckled as they started toward the building. "How many?"

"I stopped at five. Three named this movie, and I thought you'd like it because it's about a couple who meet in Europe."

So yes, this was still about a movie. And he'd taken her fascination with travel into account. He was a quick study—and thoughtful. "I'm intrigued."

He offered his hand as they walked toward the building, and she slipped hers into it. Such a natural thing, for a couple to hold hands. Yet it'd been a decade since she'd walked into a building this way. An odd mixture of warmth and self-consciousness fluttered like a giggle in her chest.

Philip's wife, Michaela, was headed for the door when they

stepped through. She had her three-year-old, Harmony, on her hip, and five-year-old Grace clutched her hand. With her hair up, little makeup on, and sweats—trendy sweats, but still—no one who didn't know her would recognize Michaela as a pop star. On seeing them, she beamed. "Look who it is!"

Grace waved to Gabby while clinging to her mom. Harmony tipped her head and simpered.

The one-armed hug Michaela offered prevented her from having to lower her youngest and also meant Gabby didn't have to separate from Tim.

"I didn't know you were back." Gabby had been more aware of the Millers' schedule before Philip married Michaela. Nila and Nason had been young then, and Gabby babysat. These days, the pair was old enough to watch their little sisters. Gabby hadn't been called on to help in ages, despite Michaela's travel schedule.

"I got in this morning." The young mom swept a tendril of hair away from Harmony's busy fingers, then rested her hand on Grace's head. "I stopped to see the new light fixtures, but then I heard about you two lovebirds." She pointed her grin at Tim. "Hi, by the way. You've outdone yourself, and that's saying something."

"I didn't do that much." The pink tinge on his cheeks suggested otherwise.

"Sure, you didn't." Michaela winked and bounced little Harmony, readjusting her on her hip. "He bought a license for a public showing. He's invested in this."

Tim released Gabby's hand to open the door. "You've done enough here." He tipped his head in a signal for Michaela to leave.

Eyes dancing, she stepped through. "You know I have essentially forever to tell her. She lives here. You don't."

Essentially forever. Disappointment dropped like an anchor. Perhaps she *would* be here forever.

Tim let the door close on her teasing and motioned Gabby to proceed. "Shall we?"

She crossed the dining room without being sure of their destination, but as she approached the bar, strings of patio lights came into view beyond it, in the event space. The Signalmen only played two or three times a week, and most other gigs happened on weekends, so there was no live music tonight. Instead, a handwritten sign displayed the name of a movie Gabby wasn't familiar with and a time—seven p.m.

Fifteen minutes from now.

A trio of older ladies from Gabby's church chattered in line at a popcorn machine. Five couches formed loose rows. Another couple took seats in the row before the stage, where a sheet served as a screen. Many Oaks didn't have a theater, but Tim had created one. To think he had offered to let her back out—and she almost had.

She could kiss him for his thoughtfulness. Or that might be too forward. But ...

You only live once. Wasn't that what the kids said? Or used to say anyway? Aunt Gladys would agree. She threaded her arm through his and tipped up to press a quick kiss to his cheek.

His eyes lit and lines of surprise formed across his forehead. He inhaled as though to say something, but instead tilted his head, studying her with amusement.

She squeezed his arm. "This is really special. Thank you."

As THE MOVIE ENDED, Gabby relished the warm weight of Tim's arm around her shoulders. But then the room brightened. Someone had turned the strings of patio lights back on, disrupting the semi-privacy they'd enjoyed during the movie. Next, the trio of seventy-something ladies rose. One fixed her gaze on Gabby, eyebrows hiked.

When she turned away and started whispering to one of her companions, who promptly looked over too, Gabby straightened her spine. She didn't want to dive into the dating pool with witnesses any more than she'd have liked diving into a swimming pool under scrutiny.

Tim dropped his arm. "What'd you think?"

Lots of things, the least important of which was the self-consciousness. She pulled her focus back to the thrill of connection. Tim had gone to so much trouble. The characters' all-nighter exploring the streets of Brussels had added a new city to her bucket list. Even so, less jealousy tinged her desire to go than she'd normally experience. After all, she was on her own magical date. "Tonight's been truly wonderful. Thank you."

He grinned like all of his artists had produced chart-topping songs.

The last two couples called their thanks.

Tim waved an acknowledgment as they made their way out, leaving her and Tim alone in the large room.

Scooting to the edge of her seat, she clasped her knees. The Depot used this room several nights a week, and the community center's popcorn and projection machines needed to be returned. These plush couches must have homes expecting them back as well. "Can I help clean up?"

"That's my project for tomorrow. Philip doesn't need the room until Blaze's next show. Speaking of ..." His focus roamed her face. As though what he saw pleased him, his lips tipped up. "You want to join me?"

A delicious curl of attraction unfurled in her core. She hadn't been admired so openly or by someone she was attracted to in return in ages. "I'd love to."

He tucked a lock of her hair behind her ear. The trail of skin he'd touched tingled, and the place where he rested his fingertips against her neck warmed. His attention drifted to her lips. Was he going to kiss her? Excitement fluttered in her lungs, and she held her breath until she trusted it to flow normally.

What was dating protocol? Did it apply? She and Tim had less than a week together. Should they take advantage of the time they had or not get carried away?

Tim's lashes lifted, his focus returning to her eyes. He touched her cheek, then dropped his hand and rose to shut down the laptop.

Gabby exhaled long and slow. She'd forgotten the dizzying exhilaration of a new romance. No wonder people inquired about her love life. How had she lived without one for so long?

The answer was obvious. Tim hadn't been around to intrigue her and treat her to grand gestures. But if she needed to stay in Many Oaks, she couldn't have a relationship with him. At least, not long-term. Short-term, though? She'd enjoy his company while she had it. If he'd kissed her, she would've soaked up every moment of it with however much of her brain hadn't vaporized from pure giddiness.

She wiped her hands on her thighs as she stood. "Too bad there isn't as much to see here as in Brussels."

Tim hit a button, and the laptop screen darkened. "They would've enjoyed Many Oaks just as much. The city was just a backdrop." He unplugged the cord connecting the laptop and the projector. He looped it into a coil as he spared her a meaningful glance. "The main attraction was the company."

"So you're game for a ..." Movement beyond him drew Gabby's attention before she extended the invitation to spend the evening walking the town.

Isabella took a seat at the bar, turning to observe her father. Charity stood beside her, arms crossed and chewing her lip as though uncertain whether to approach or disappear.

Gabby had asked for a few days. She'd calmed down since, but what should she say to her daughter? Charity looked the picture of remorse, and though Gabby was hurt and worried, she refused to leave her daughter in agony.

Tim followed her line of sight, then turned back to the laptop. "If it isn't the pair of prodigals." He spoke quietly enough that the girls wouldn't hear.

Gabby lifted her purse. She regretted the interruption as much as he seemed to, but Charity deserved priority. "How do we love them when we disapprove of their choices?"

"The two aren't mutually exclusive."

"They *can* be mutually destructive." She tangled her fingers in the straps of her purse, judging her options. "Love fiercely, disagree gently."

Tim closed the laptop lid. "That's your plan?"

She rounded the loveseat and table, nearing him, and they looked toward the girls together. "Got a better one?"

"Nope. Disagreeing persistently hasn't changed anything for me and Issy." As if on cue, his daughter stood and started for them. Tim fit his arm around Gabby's shoulders. "Never considered gentleness."

Gabby threaded her arm behind his waist, returning the side hug. "It's not too late to give it a try."

He gave a gentle squeeze, then let her go. "Not so sure." He collected the laptop, then eyed their daughters. He must've judged the waning distance still adequate. "I've been thinking a lot about legacy lately, but I might've missed my chance at a positive one with her years ago."

"No way." Gabby brushed his hand as she took the first step toward her own daughter. "It's not too late. It's now or never."

8

———————

"**I** do not like being lied to." He also didn't like his date being interrupted. Yet Tim hadn't raised his voice. Did the restraint count as gentle?

Isabella had driven their rented SUV to The Depot, but Tim took the wheel for the trip to the house. Elbow propped on the center console, she flicked her fingers. "It was for your own good. We gave you plausible deniability."

"How would you like me making decisions that I think are for your good?"

"Don't you dare."

Too late. His conscience stung. He'd justified his omission about his health by telling himself she was better off coming on the trip. Without an intervention, she'd be in his place in another twenty-five or thirty years, trying to turn her child's life around before the cycle repeated yet again.

The thought of a grandkid slammed the brakes on his thoughts. He caught his foot a moment before hitting the actual brakes.

A grandchild. He'd step up as a grandfather. Even so, the

child would be hers. Isabella's childhood wounds would impact everything unless he turned this around.

The whole idea might be a moot point. Did young couples these days still dream of starting families? He'd never seen Isabella take an interest in babies or toddlers. Then again, they didn't run into many.

"Are you and Lars going to have kids?"

"If this is your way of asking if I'm pregnant, the answer's no."

"I'm asking where you two stand." They wouldn't be talking marriage if they hadn't discussed something as basic as their desire, or lack thereof, for kids. Right?

"We stand nowhere. We're young. There'll be plenty of time to decide later."

"Accidents happen." Gabby had lost her husband to one. Tim, himself, had been in a car wreck earlier this year. To check him for internal injuries, they'd completed an abdominal CT scan. The tumor they'd found by pure accident could've cut his life short, had it been cancerous. While his prognosis was great, the scare had forced the knowledge that his days were numbered.

You're lucky you're dying. Isabella's words on arriving in Many Oaks echoed in his mind.

His chest ached. He didn't think he'd ever feel ready to step from an existence he knew to one he wouldn't fully understand until he got there. However, knowing the clock was ticking was a blessing in a way. One didn't waste a limited resource. In theory.

"Lars and I have been living together for months already. No *accidents*"—she made finger quotes—"have happened."

"I didn't mean a pregnancy. I meant you don't always have as much time as you think you will. And even if you do, I've learned the hard way it's easier to waste than you might expect."

"You're saying you wasted your life?" Her dry tone conveyed a smirk, but he didn't look over to verify.

"Would you say I've used it well?" He turned onto their street, praying for a breakthrough.

"Are you really asking?" Her shock seemed like a step in the right direction.

"Yeah. Tell me. Have I used my life well?"

Silence stretched, and then a soft question. "Is this because you're afraid of cancer?"

"No." He shifted in his seat. The doctor had told him he didn't need to worry about it, and he was choosing to believe him. Hopefully, when they opened him up, they wouldn't find any more surprises. Maybe the possibility, small as it was, justified not telling Isabella the biopsy results. "Something worse."

"What?"

"Just answer the question. Have I used my life well?" He glanced at her.

Illuminated by passing streetlights, a shrug jolted her shoulders. "You're successful."

"At what?"

"Your career." Her hand fluttered midair. "Financially. I've seen you on entertainment shows and tabloids." She snorted. "Though I'm not sure photobombing Awestruck counts as success."

Cute. Journalists had sought him out on red carpets and quoted him in music industry publications, but why brag about it? "I've used my life on my career."

"You date some too. And go to church. Read the paper ..."

Before she digressed into even more mundane tasks, he jumped in. "And that's a good use? In your mind?"

"I don't know what you want from me." Her volume had quieted.

"I want you to see the mistakes I made so you understand why I'm trying to be different. Music comes and goes. Only the best songs survive in the public consciousness more than a couple of years, but relationships impact generations. They're a person's true legacy. Awestruck has made a lasting difference in people's lives—eternal, even—but that's them, not me. In my most important relationship, I've been absent, and I want to do better."

"And your idea of better is talking me out of marrying Lars? Dad, it's my life."

"Remember when you dyed your hair green?" He had video-called her at boarding school the day after the failed attempt to turn her blonde hair blue. She'd tried to hide the mishap with a hat, but the knit must've been itchy, because she pushed it aside partway through their conversation, revealing the grassy color of her locks.

"You are not comparing my fiancé to a botched dye job."

Sort of. "If your daughter comes home with a box of blue hair dye, what will you do?"

"Take her to a professional. But you didn't even know I bought it because—"

"You lived in a dorm." She'd begged to attend the school because of its acting program. He'd enrolled her before coming to Christ. Afterward, she'd enjoyed the school so much, he hadn't had the heart to insist she come home, even though he'd known his priorities ought to change.

He silently asked God to forgive him for failing to be the father he should've been. He hit the garage door remote as the house came into view. "So you'd stop her from repeating your mistakes."

"You're comparing both my fiancé *and* my mom to blue hair dye."

Tim turned into the driveway. "Our marriage was hurried and brief, and we caused a lot of pain."

"You also caused me."

"*You're* not blue hair dye." Once in the garage, he shifted into park. "You're the one part of this that isn't."

"Nice save." Isabella rolled her eyes.

"Back then, I didn't have anyone telling me things could be different." He'd discovered Awestruck a few years later, and their good example had taken over a decade to sink in. "It's not an excuse for how I acted. I just don't want you as lost as I was."

"So now I'm lost."

What a trainwreck. Tim got out, rounded the vehicle, and opened Isabella's door. She remained seated and leaned away in a half-hearted recoil, but he took her hand and waited until she met his eyes.

His little girl, the one whose pictures he'd stared at with longing on holidays, the one he had foolishly—so foolishly—allowed to grow up without him, was in there. Somewhere. She'd hidden under layers of maturity, hurt, and independence, but she was still in there. She had to be.

Isabella looked at him, eyes round with uncertainty.

"I love you, Isabella. You are the best part of my life and the only part of my legacy that matters."

Her bottom lip trembled. The emotion meant she hadn't heard this from him often enough and perhaps didn't believe him. Her doubt cut deeply.

His voice thickened. "I want you to be happier than I've ever been."

She frowned at him for the space of two breaths. "You could start by trusting me to make good decisions." Her hands pulled from his. "And reaching out even when you're not worried."

If she went ahead with marrying Lars, that time may never come. Trusting her with the choice felt like surrendering to defeat. Yet, his Heavenly Father had allowed him his mistakes. Didn't he owe his adult daughter the same freedom? "Okay. You're right. It is your life, and I've overstepped. I'm sorry."

A line appeared between Isabella's eyebrows. "You are?"

He nodded and stepped back, allowing her space to exit the vehicle. "If you want to go, I'll buy you a ticket back to New York."

She joined him in the garage and shut the SUV door, her movements slow. After studying him, she shook her head. "No, I miss him, but we're here. It's only a few days' difference, and there's more to do than I expected."

Tim swallowed another complaint about her part in deceiving Gabby. They'd already discussed it, and he'd trust her to not repeat the error. "I did appreciate your help today." He held the door and followed her into the galley-style kitchen, an idea brewing.

Isabella might be willing to stay in Many Oaks, but she'd enjoy it more with Lars' company. Besides, time together might help Tim bond with the guy. He'd reach out to Lars tomorrow, see if he would come if Tim provided the ticket.

Isabella lingered at the counter. "What are you going to do with all the couches at The Depot?"

He'd bought them from the clearance section of a furniture store two towns over. "Sell them on social media?"

"Even if we find buyers before we leave, you'll never make back as much as you spent." She slipped her phone from her pocket. She often doublechecked such theories, and Tim assumed that's what she was doing as she typed, then started to scroll. "Do you always spend so much on your dates?"

"Definitely not." Dinner and a show, even in LA, would've cost less, but he'd made the mistake of renting the projector and popcorn maker first. Only later did he learn how much movie licensing cost.

Then came seating decisions. The Depot's chairs served their purpose, but a movie required more comfort. A more fiscally responsible planner might have commandeered all the office chairs in a three-mile radius, but he'd wanted to sit close to Gabby. Besides, he'd already invested hundreds in the night. Might as well see it through.

In the end, he could've bought Gabby a ticket to see Europe firsthand for the same price. But she would've recognized the price tag and refused. The beauty of tonight's date was that the extravagance flew under the radar.

Correction: the beauty of it was Gabby had enjoyed herself.

"You're in love, huh?" Isabella lowered her phone without commenting on her search, a sign she'd been right about the market for used furniture.

The compulsive part of him wanted to say yes, but he knew better. Perhaps his daughter didn't, and that was why she'd agreed to marry Lars. "There's a big difference between initial excitement and love."

Isabella brushed the countertop, clearing away nonexistent crumbs.

Tim held his breath. Was she thinking about Lars more reasonably? He had to know. "You okay?"

She stilled. "Just, um ..." She frowned at him, then resumed her study of her fingers. "I'm sorry about trying to cover up Charity's plan. It was silly of her to think her mom wouldn't find out. And, um, while I'm apologizing, I shouldn't have said what I did when we got here. I hope the biopsy comes back clear."

"Thanks. Look ..." He needed to tell her the results so she'd stop worrying. But telling her could sever the tenuous threads that had joined them together for this trip.

Before he landed on a suitable response, her phone rang.

She checked the display and turned. "Don't worry about it. I'm sure it'll be fine." She answered the call as she shut herself into her room.

Tomorrow. He'd tell her tomorrow.

~

Gabby's coffee table and mounds of conflict separated her from her youngest daughter.

Charity's gaze darted across the chasm and dropped. "You think I'm ruining my life."

Gabby unleashed a deep breath and a prayer for the wisdom to answer her daughter. "I think living with a man you're not married to is a mistake, and it could have major consequences, but ..." Charity might interpret her response as permission to spiral further. Or the truth would bridge the gap between them. "I don't think a life is that easy to ruin."

Charity's shoulders inched away from her ears, and the lock her arms had formed seemed to loosen.

"Still." Gabby dipped her chin, up to her neck in doubts. "I don't understand. Why take the relationship to this level?"

The question undid the little progress she'd made as Charity's posture hardened again. "We make a good team. He listens, he's steady, and he loves me."

"Is he a believer?" The choice to live together suggested an answer, but even Christians got off track sometimes. Just look at King David. He'd repented when confronted with his sin. If Charity and Reese shared a common faith, perhaps Gabby might help them do the same.

"No." Charity sank back farther into Gabby's living room couch. Her refusal to make eye contact served as a shield. "I'm not anymore, either."

Feeling as if she were being tossed around by airplane turbulence, Gabby clutched the armrests of her chair. Once, another mother at church had said that because her son had trusted Jesus when he was young, his eternity was still secure, though he denied the faith as an adult. Gabby didn't share that mother's confidence. Still, maybe. Theologians argued both sides, so who was she to say?

The unknown lent little comfort.

How had it come to this?

Charity hadn't explained her choice to withdraw from church, even when asked. Left to draw her own conclusions, Gabby had attributed Charity's choice to carelessness, not disbelief. Hoping her daughter would come back around, Gabby had sprinkled references to faith, church, and Bible verses in their conversations. Though drawing her back wouldn't be as easy as she'd hoped, God could still work. Gabby silently begged Him to.

"See?" Charity groaned. "This is why I didn't tell you."

Because she was shocked? Hurt? Scared? "When did this change? And why?" Her mouth felt clumsy.

Charity wore an old T-shirt and jeans today, casual clothes suitable for helping someone move. Her shrug shifted the logo of her alma matter across her chest. "The Bible says God is good, but a lot of the stuff He does proves otherwise."

"Like Dad's accident?"

The loss had been traumatic for all of them, but Charity and Natalie had continued attending church and youth group. They'd seemed to grow in their walks with the Lord. At least, when they lost Judah, none of them had lost faith.

Or so Gabby had thought.

Charity's pinkening nose signaled rising emotion. Instead of allowing tears to fall, a sneer overtook her face. "Do you know how many people told me good would come of it? Like it was a blessing. Like God wanted it to happen."

"Death is part of the curse, sweetheart. Humanity chose it, not God."

Her red eyes cast a fleeting glance at Gabby and returned to scowling at the coffee table. "If He's in control of everything, then He chooses when and how it happens. He chose to cut Dad's life short. I refuse to trust a God like that."

Gabby ran her hands over her thighs—the very lap four-year-old Charity had sat on as she'd prayed to ask Jesus to forgive her sins and lead her life.

"A semi driver runs a stop sign and kills Dad and everyone wants to make sense of it, but it's *non*sensical." Charity's roughened voice plowed on. "And when I point that out, they dismiss it with some quip about how God's ways aren't our ways." She rolled her eyes. "They can say that again."

"I understand why you're angry. I dealt with a lot of anger too."

"What's the answer?" This time, her glance lingered a few seconds before falling again.

That Charity would ask such a question and wait for a reply gave her hope. Perhaps God would use this conversation to break through years of pain and doubt. *Please, Lord.*

"You're right. God did allow the accident and did allow Dad to die. To us, it is nonsensical."

"To us." Charity put mocking emphasis on the words as she repeated them. A red flush crept up her neck. "But to God, it all makes sense, and we're just supposed to be grateful."

"We live in a fallen world. There's heartbreak here, but you can bring your pain and anger to God. Your struggles aren't too much for Him. Mine weren't." She measured her words, praying God would fill in each idea as she needed it. "What eventually comforted me was that, in light of eternity, this life is just vapor. It's not where we're supposed to store up all our hopes and dreams."

Gabby had put a lot of stock in her dream of travel and bundles of hopes in her daughters' lives. If her concern hadn't been so zoomed in on the temporal, she might've seen the battle for Charity's soul raging.

Well, her eyes were open now. "This life isn't the main event. When Dad died young, all he did was flip past the prologue. He advanced to the best part of the story in a book that never ends."

Charity chewed the corner of her mouth.

"I don't expect what I say to satisfy you." Not expecting it didn't stop her from pleading for the Lord to make it so. "The things people said after the accident didn't help, but not necessarily because they were wrong. The problem is, truth delivered that way is too sudden. It's like taking a tree from a nursery, setting it on top of the dirt without digging in first, and expecting it to take root."

Her daughter's jaw ticked. Not following? Not impressed?

The analogy quickened Gabby's pulse. She trusted God had prompted it, so she continued. "It's the slow, hard-earned epiphanies that heal us. Seeds of truth need time and care to get established in the unique soil of a soul. We water them with prayer, study, and hard conversations, but God causes the growth."

"He didn't for me."

"Have you asked Him to?"

"Back in high school. I don't remember the exact words, but I tried." Her throat marked a swallow, and when she spoke again, she did so more softly. "If God's real, I don't trust Him. I'm done."

In periods of doubt and struggle, Gabby had never doubted God's existence or given up on her faith. She'd found that if she continued attending church and spending time with God and with His people, He would, in time, comfort and heal.

Charity seemed bent on severing the relationship instead. Gabby would trade every one of her dreams if it meant she could stop her.

9

Tim's conscience weighed more than the couch he and Isabella had just helped load into the back of some guy's pickup. He needed to come clean, and since he'd invited Lars to Iowa, he needed to do it soon, before the third wheel arrived. He resisted rubbing his lower back as the buyer shut his tailgate.

"Thanks again!" The guy passed Tim a wad of cash and hopped in the cab.

Tim slid the bills into his wallet, heart hammering a drumroll as he built up to the truth. The whole truth. "Lunch?"

"Here?" Isabella had the courtesy to not sound disappointed, despite having eaten at The Depot yesterday too.

"I'd like to hear the band. That okay?" The music hall here would be empty, save for Blaze and The Signalmen's rehearsal. Tim could break his news with fewer witnesses. If things went okay, he'd have the bonus of a behind-the-scenes look at Blaze and The Signalmen.

"I guess the air conditioning is as good here as anywhere."

At least Tim wasn't the only one winded by ridding the event hall of couches. Only one had sold. Tim, Isabella, Philip, and Nason, Philip's son, had stashed the rest of them in Philip's garage. If they didn't interest buyers before Tim left town, Philip could burn them for all Tim cared. He—and his back, especially—had had enough of lugging them from one place to another.

Inside, Tim took the lead with the hostess. "Can we get a table in the event hall?"

The teenager behind the podium dropped her gaze to the seating chart. "Let me see ..."

David crossed behind her with a tray of drinks. On spotting Isabella, he stopped and the liquid sloshed toward the rims. "How are my favorite tourists?"

"David!" Isabella greeted him like a long-lost friend.

What was with this guy waiting tables, anyway? Gabby said he was a military veteran. Didn't he have usable skills from his time in the service?

Of course such things wouldn't bother his daughter. She and Lars had been under-employed since the end of the Broadway show that was supposed to have been their big break.

David peered over the hostess's shoulder. "You can seat them in my section."

"They asked for a table in back." The hostess whispered out the corner of her mouth, as though they wouldn't overhear.

"No problem. They're friends of Philip's, and I can serve them there."

Great. If his conversation with Issy flopped, good ol' David would be a witness. Was it too late to suggest they eat at the rental? The hostess was already leading the way to the back, Isabella following.

Tim would have to make the best of it.

On stage in back, Blaze held a microphone, but they'd left the sound system turned down. He wouldn't pick up nuances of their performance from here, but he could observe whether everyone worked well together—if his conversation with Isabella allowed him to turn his attention.

He and Isabella sat, and the hostess distributed the menus. After a nervous glance toward Philip, she hurried away.

"Poor girl thinks she's going to lose her job over this." Isabella chuckled. "Should've told her you're a big shot."

"Only to a certain set of people."

If anyone onstage had noticed their arrival, they'd ignored it as the emotional heart of the song reached its crescendo. Blaze had talent. Did she also have the business sense required to succeed in music? He'd have to talk to her to find out. And then there was the question of whether Million Dollar Ransom had her beat. Philip wouldn't have vouched for them without good reason.

When David materialized, Tim ordered, then checked an incoming text.

I should get there around eight, Lars had written.

Movement drew Tim's attention up as Isabella passed David her menu. His brush of her hand didn't look accidental. Isabella flashed a quick smile of thanks, then picked up her soda as though she'd thought nothing of it.

Indignation on Lars's behalf fought with his desire for a clear conscience. He didn't like the guy, but he liked the idea of Isabella being unfaithful to him even less. Especially since a player like David did not seem like the lesser of two evils.

"Does she have star potential?" Isabella propped her head against her hand, scrunching her cheek upward.

Stalling, Tim refocused on stage. "She's got the voice, stage presence, and a good local following."

"And good music." Isabella tapped her thumb on the table to the beat. "Although it's no wonder she has a local following. There can't be many singers here."

Talking music was so much easier than talking about his

health, but his conscience was stomping around again. "Look, I need to tell—"

"I used to wish—"

Tim motioned his daughter to continue. He and Issy hadn't talked much about her dreams since she'd first started pining after a Broadway career at age fourteen.

"I used to wish I was a rock star. I even started a band, if you can believe it."

"A band?" Tim cut a glance at the stage, trying to imagine Isabella with the microphone or a guitar. Piano? Had her mom ever gotten her lessons as a kid?

Isabella shrugged, lazy focus on the musicians. She had loved theater since Tim had gotten to know her as a young teen. Even after he'd enrolled her in the boarding school that specialized in the performing arts, she'd begged for private acting and voice lessons. Since he'd traveled so much, his guilt had inspired him to oblige. But the kind of musical performance she'd studied varied greatly from the kind he represented.

"At what age?" he asked.

"Um, like, eight." She assessed him as though reading his questions. "I thought you'd spend time with me."

"If you had a band?" Even before the answer, the pieces fit into a sad picture of their relationship.

"Mom told me about your job." Her nonchalant tone chipped at his heart. She'd once been desperate for his attention, and he'd been absent.

He cleared the lump from his throat. "I'm sorry for who I was."

She traced her finger in circles on the tabletop, seemingly mesmerized.

"I wish I'd heard your band."

She snickered. "No, you don't. None of us had any idea how

to play any instruments, besides the one girl who knew Chopsticks."

"What did you play?"

"Tambourine. Except we didn't have a tambourine, so I shook a bell we found under someone's couch." She jiggled her hand in the air. "We practiced twice, I think."

"All to see me."

She lifted her chin like she was looking down her nose at her younger self. "That was part of it, anyway."

"People do crazy things for family."

"Yeah, maybe."

"Definitely." He shoved himself onward. Isabella deserved better from him, and he'd start immediately. "I did something wrong to convince you to come on this road trip."

She cocked her head, still facing toward the stage more than toward him, and shifted her line of sight, giving him the epitome of side eyes. "Oh?"

"This time together is important to me. Some of our last real father-daughter time."

She swiveled on her seat to face him, one hand clutching the edge of the table. "Did the biopsy come back cancerous? Before the trip even started? You should've told—"

He motioned to cut her off before she stressed herself out with more terrible guesses. "It came back *pre*cancerous."

"Oh." Her face froze a moment before her brow furrowed.

"The prognosis is great. They plan to laparoscopically remove the part of my pancreas with the tumor. It'll mean a few days in the hospital and a few weeks of recovery, but barring any surprises, the operation should resolve it."

"No chemo or anything?"

He shook his head.

"So it's good news."

He nodded. "I should've told you. I'm sorry I let you worry so much longer than you needed to. I was afraid you wouldn't come on the trip, and I didn't want my legacy to be one of missed opportunities and neglect. But hiding the truth was selfish of me." He'd rather keep rambling than listen to her vent her frustration with him, but that too would be selfish. He fell quiet.

Micro expressions zipped across Isabella's features. A couple flinches looked angry, one thoughtful, another sad. Her blue eyes locked on him. "You could've told me."

He nodded. "*Should've* told you."

"I still would've come."

"Really?" He shouldn't question her when he was the one in the doghouse, but it slipped out.

"Yeah. Sure." She chewed her bottom lip and shifted to pull her phone from her back pocket. Looking at the screen, she frowned. Had she even unlocked it? Perhaps there was a troubling text preview on the lock screen.

"Hey, Tim!" Philip called from the stage.

When had rehearsal ended? Several minutes ago, at least, since the guitarists and drummer were already exiting.

Philip motioned him forward, toward Blaze. "Come on up. I'll introduce you."

As if he could leave Isabella.

She pushed away from the table. "I'm sorry. I forgot." She stood, stuffing the phone away again. "There's somewhere I'm supposed to be." She licked her lips, but instead of stammering through another excuse, she tipped her head to point his attention toward the stage. Or, rather, something approaching from that direction—Philip headed over, Blaze a couple of steps behind him with her purse over her shoulder.

When Tim looked back, Isabella was already several steps away, on her way to the exit.

"Wait." The weak request didn't deter her.

What had happened? Was she angry? She'd hadn't had the flash-bang reaction he'd expected.

Footsteps neared the table, and he turned to find Philip and Blaze standing across from him.

"Tim, I'd like you to meet Blaze Astley."

He rose and shot one last glance after Isabella. Obviously, she didn't want to talk to him.

He focused on the artist. "I heard about you within five minutes of arriving, and I have to say, there's something to the rumors."

Blaze accepted the compliment with a gentle smile and an extended hand. "And I have no doubt there's something to the rumors about your work with Awestruck." She exuded confidence from her posture to her even tone to her firm handshake.

He motioned to the seats across from himself. "You play other venues or just here?"

Blaze held up a hand to refuse the chair, and they all remained standing. "I have to get back to work. But we do other gigs on Saturdays when The Depot is booked for special events."

"I don't travel." Philip braced his hands on the back of a chair. "We have another bassist who fills in. They've gone as far north as the Twin Cities and south to Kansas City, plus they've done a few fairs and outdoor festivals. Ninety percent of those are gigs Blaze hustled up."

She took a sideways step like she might sneak out mid-conversation. "Every time we get out, we promote our email list. With more signups, it's easier to spread the word about shows, which makes shows easier to book."

Interesting. Smart. The strategy would be one of Tim's first recommendations if they weren't already using it. Since they were, Tim glanced to Philip to gauge his involvement.

Philip lifted his hands, signaling he'd kept out of it.

Blaze was becoming more intriguing by the minute. A lot of questions remained to be answered, though. "You're looking to make this a full-time gig?"

"As much as I'd love to, I'm not cut out for the big leagues. And if I don't hustle, I'm going to be late for my real job." With a quick wave, she made a beeline for the exit.

Gaping, Tim watched her flight. "What's this job she's rushing off to?"

A chuckle rumbled in Philip's throat. "She's a car salesman ... Person. Sales*person*. Sells more than her two counterparts put together, but then, she's motivated."

"By what?"

"She has custody of her sister. That's why she won't pursue music. She can't travel much or take a risk with her income."

Other artists made it work. Philip had for a time. Michaela had young kids and traveled, but she had family to rely on. If Blaze had custody of a sister, the parents weren't in the picture. "How old's the girl?"

"Mercy's going into sixth grade in the fall."

"There are online school options. She could study on the road."

Philip shrugged. "It's not me you have to convince."

A good thing, since Tim had failed to talk Philip into staying with Awestruck. Philip decided the best course for his family was for him to quit the band and move back to his hometown.

"Tell me you don't miss it sometimes."

Philip shook his head with an exaggerated frown. "God's blessed me immensely since I listened when He said to quit. I got to build something here—a family, a business, and I still get to play with the band most days. That's the best of all worlds."

Tim stuffed his hand in his pocket. How would God have blessed him if he'd listened to the prompt to find a way to keep Isabella close during her teen years instead of leaving her at boarding school?

If he had, she wouldn't have connected with the casting director who helped her land a role in the Broadway play. She also wouldn't have met Lars. Would she want to trade? How would their relationship look today if he'd been more attentive earlier?

As Philip headed off, Tim reclaimed his seat. *What ifs* would paralyze him if he camped out there. He prayed for the hundredth time that God would heal the wounds left by his choice and pulled out his phone to attempt being part of the solution.

Are we okay? Are you okay? Without sending the message, he squinted at the words. Was that the best he could do? Was it appropriate?

He jolted when a plate clunked onto the table in front of him. Lunch.

David set Isabella's food across from him. "Need anything else?"

He hated to admit to this punk that his daughter had ditched him, but unless he ate a smokehouse burger *and* a chicken sandwich, the guy would learn the truth. Might as well come out with it.

"Can you box Isabella's? Something came up."

David's eyebrows hiked toward his hairline. "Ah ... sure." The waiter whisked the plate away, and Tim went back to his text.

He wasn't a wordsmith. He sent the message, sat back in his seat, and stared at his burger. He should've asked David for two boxes.

10

———

ood thing Tim had found a table in the event hall before eight o'clock, because as showtime arrived, people claimed the last ones.

No Gabby yet. No Lars. No Isabella.

Blaze joined The Signalmen on stage and kicked off the night with an original.

If only Tim didn't have so much to juggle, he'd listen. He watched the entrance anxiously, wondering who'd walk in first. He didn't want to admit to Lars that he had no idea where his daughter was, but he hadn't seen her since she'd left their lunch earlier. He also didn't want to ditch Gabby for as long as it might take to resolve whatever was going on with Isabella. After all, it was already Wednesday. Gabby would be busy with Natalie's arrival tomorrow and her birthday party on Friday night.

Still, he'd prioritize Isabella. If she came around.

A steadying hand smoothed across his shoulder blades. "Sorry to keep you waiting." Gabby slid into the seat beside him, so close her arm pressed against his.

He shifted, resting his arm across the back of her chair. "Crazy day?"

"Not so much crazy as ..." She blew out a long breath. "I think I have an emotional hangover from talking to Charity last night."

Tim winced. "That bad, huh?" They'd texted earlier, so he knew it hadn't gone well, but no details.

"She told me she's not a Christian anymore." The music almost drowned out the confession, despite how close she sat.

What could he say? That their daughters were temperamental and beyond comprehension? True, but unhelpful. "You must be devastated."

Gabby gave a shell-shocked nod. "I don't know what to do."

"Love fiercely, disagree gently?"

"If only that would change her mind."

Tim didn't mean to shift his focus from her, but bright red appeared in the background. Lars. Leave it to a theater guy to wear a shirt that could double as a matador's cape. He'd rented a car at the airport. Tim had directed him to meet them at The Depot, hoping Isabella would show up.

"I miss my little girl." Gabby peered in Lars's direction, too, and it took Tim a moment to realize she wasn't looking at Lars, but at Charity. She and her friends were about ten feet beyond Lars, at the bar.

Isabella wasn't among them. In a matter of seconds, Lars would come to him instead.

Tim shifted closer to Gabby and ran his fingertips over her arm. "I was set against faith, and I came around. Charity's story isn't over yet."

Gabby tipped her head onto his shoulder. He rested his cheek against her crown and inhaled the scents of fruit and flowers that infused her hair. So captivated by the softness against his cheek, he didn't even notice he'd let his eyes sink closed until he opened them again and found that the red shirt had gotten larger—Lars had spotted him and was approaching.

Tim would've waited for him in place, but Gabby straightened in her seat and gave him a grateful, if a little sheepish, smile.

He rubbed her back. "You'll be just fine, and Charity is in good hands—God's."

A long exhale breezed through her lips.

Lars was two tables away now.

"Excuse me one minute." Tim pushed away from the table, stood, and met the actor.

"Hey. Is she here somewhere?" Lars's furrowed brow pushed on the bridge of his glasses as he scanned the room. Shoulders hunched, he didn't look like a man excited to see his fiancée. He looked ... afraid.

Of Tim?

They'd interacted little. Tim hadn't liked the guy, but he'd been civil. He'd thought. Maybe Isabella had told Lars horror stories about him. Like how he'd talked for a hundred miles about why they shouldn't get married. He tried to relax the confusion and judgment from his features. "Haven't seen her yet. Have you tried her cell?"

Lars's gaze darted to Tim. "I thought this was a surprise."

Isabella was constantly on her phone. Surely she'd been complaining about Tim all day. Lars ought to know she was avoiding Tim. He also should've been able to ascertain her whereabouts.

But this was the man Isabella loved, and Tim had vowed to do better. He aimed his attention at his phone and messaged Isabella. *Haven't heard from you all day, and your friends are at The Depot. Where are you?*

A response might not be coming. Even if it was, how long did he want to entertain Lars? At the bar, Charity sipped a drink, watching the stage instead of Reese, who stood by her side and—based on his movements—was telling some story that involved ducking and weaving. Maybe Charity could help.

Tim crossed the distance.

She acknowledged him with a lackluster smile.

"Do you know where Isabella is?"

Charity's line of sight ticked toward Lars. No wonder, since in that shirt, he stood out like Rudolph among all the other reindeer.

Might as well explain. Knowing he was doing Isabella a favor might get him an answer. "Her fiancé's come to visit."

Her whole head dipped forward as though she'd lost her balance for a moment. "Her fiancé?"

Hopefully Isabella would show more joy when the surprise was revealed or she'd scare Lars right back to New York City. Tim thumbed toward the guy, pointing him out since he'd hung back. "Lars."

"I see." Charity traced the bottom of her glass with her finger. "She's around here somewhere."

"You sure? I haven't seen her."

"She's not avoiding *me*."

That could mean the girls had talked, or Charity could be misleading him.

He thanked her anyway and rejoined Lars. "Her friend says she's here. If you can't find her, check the place we rented. I'll text you the address."

"Okay." He clapped Tim on the shoulder. "I hope it'll work out."

Work out? What did that mean?

Lars headed into the crowd without saying more. Issy sure knew how to pick 'em.

❧

EVEN BLAZE'S performance failed to captivate Gabby. She fidgeted as Tim spoke with Charity.

Her daughter, whom she loved.

Her daughter, whom she'd failed.

Tears rose.

You cannot take responsibility for another person's choices.

The stern thought checked the tears but didn't cure her guilt. Parents influenced their children. If she'd done something differently, Charity might've made other choices. If only Gabby's presence in Many Oaks had been the positive influence she'd intended.

Miserable, she pulled up the website of the staffing agency she'd planned to work with. She refreshed the search for relevant positions. One in Orange, California, topped the list.

She blinked, but the location didn't change. Orange was close to LA. Close to Tim. Hope and fear wrung her heart. Was this position's appearance a divine nudge? Did He want her to go because she'd failed with Charity? Or to free her from a losing battle? The moisture seeped back into her eyes.

The self-condemnation needed to stop. God was bigger than her mistakes, and Charity's future was in His hands. He would have His way.

Besides, this nudge to travel wasn't new. She'd been delaying for months while she "helped" Charity. All her efforts had been in vain. Perhaps God had wanted her to leave before now? Although He must've known she'd drag her feet—He was all-knowing—so maybe He'd sent Tim and given her another reason, a fun reason, to relocate.

Orange's proximity to LA would allow her to visit Tim when he was in town. How often was that? The connection she'd ruled out as impossible could become meaningful.

She'd also always wanted to live in a warmer climate. She'd never miss scraping ice and snow off her car after shifts, but would she find equal joy in a snowless Christmas? How did Tim celebrate the holidays?

She scrolled through the job details again.

Gabby had known she'd need a license to practice in other states, so she'd been studying to take her boards again. Still, it could take months to obtain the necessary credentials, depending on California's requirements. This exact position might be filled before then.

But if this was God, He would ensure the right position opened up at the right time.

"There are palm trees on your phone." Tim retook his seat and nestled an arm around her. "Planning a vacation?"

What would he think of the truth?

Afraid of the answer, she darkened the screen. Yet the weight of his arm around her shoulders lent comfort. A hint of spice carried on the air, adding to the intimacy of the moment.

She wanted this to last.

Unreasonable, perhaps, since she hardly knew him, but there it was.

Getting a job near him would allow this to play out, assuming the prospect of more time together didn't scare him off. This was only a second date, but somehow it felt like they'd known each other much longer.

Did he feel the connection?

There was only one way to find out. "It's a locum tenens position."

"Is that Latin for palm tree attendant?"

She'd been so wrapped up in her feelings and how much to reveal, she didn't follow until she woke the phone screen and glimpsed the stock photo again. Then she laughed. "It's a travel nurse practitioner."

"Oh. Really." He shifted against the back of his chair, enthusiasm brightening his features. "That's a thing?"

"Contracts are generally for three months and sometimes

come with the option to extend longer. Walk-in clinics and urgent cares especially need practitioners. I've been toying with the idea for a while."

"This is the idea you wanted to pursue?" With the hand draped near her shoulder, he traced a mindless line up and down her arm.

"Yes." Her throat hitched. "Once Charity was in a better place."

Tim studied her so intently that he didn't even flinch when someone bumped his chair. "You were and are a good mom."

"I did my best anyway, but ..."

"You were and are a good mom, even if you go and let your adult child be an adult. Especially then, in fact."

Gratitude for his concern and belief in her leveled out the seesaw of her emotions. "Thanks."

He squeezed her shoulders. "You'd get to work in the Caribbean somewhere?" His excitement for her sounded so genuine. As though California hadn't even occurred to him.

"I was thinking of staying in the US." She toyed with her phone. If a future wasn't on his radar, she wouldn't bring it up. "We have palm trees, too, you know. Not in Iowa. But in other states."

Tim's hand on her arm stilled for a moment, then resumed. "I believe I've seen some in California, in fact."

Was that hope in his eyes?

Her pulse quickened. Maybe she wasn't so crazy after all. "Have you?"

A sly smile grew as he nodded. "We also have mountains, desert, oceans, redwoods, movie stars, musicians, certain people related to the entertainment industry ..."

Her heartbeat in her eardrums obscured the music. "Like yourself?"

His playfulness sobered. "Since you mention it."

Her excitement muffled his words, almost as if she were

underwater. She leaned closer. "Are you asking me to come to California?"

She was close enough to read the deepening of the lines beside his eyes, the flicker of his lashes as he studied her, and the twitch of pleasure at the corner of his mouth. Close enough to kiss.

Perhaps their relationship ought to progress that far before anyone talked about relocating, yet here they were. Still had time to try it out before she packed her bags though.

He tipped his head toward the door. "Let's get some air."

To talk or for a first kiss?

When did she get so wrapped up in the physical that such questions popped into her mind? She found herself on her feet and threaded her hand around Tim's elbow for stability.

As they exited, Charity looked their way. Sadness—or regret—tinged her expression. Moving would mean a different relationship with her.

Losing Judah had changed everything.

Now, God just might use Tim's arrival to change it all again.

11

With the sun below the red-orange horizon, shades of royal blue and purple crept into the sky. The halos circling the bulbs on The Depot's porch grew more distinct, and the air had cooled a few notches. On a night like this, Tim could spend hours with Gabby on the wrought-iron-and-wood bench beside The Depot's doors.

Instead of following his lead to the seat on the porch, Gabby took a tentative step toward the steps that descended to the lot. "Come with me?"

"Gladly." He took her outstretched hand, ready to follow anywhere. Hard to believe they'd only known each other since Monday. After his disastrous relationship with Isabella's mom, he'd thought he'd put his days of falling hard and fast behind him.

Gabby started for the side of The Depot.

He had history, but he'd grown in the last twenty years. Become a believer. And look at him, taking time to reflect instead of immediately campaigning for her to move. Was his desire to have her close by selfish, or would she enjoy her life there, regardless of what happened between them? Was California where God wanted her?

Gabby led him behind the building. A trio of picnic benches and a small playground stood at the edge of a field. Around its edge, he caught sight of homes.

She directed her steps toward the tables but motioned toward the equipment, which included a jungle gym, a playhouse with a slide, and swings. "Philip's first act as owner was to install the play area. He worked out here while Nason and Nila played. These days, Grace, Harmony, and the neighborhood kids have taken it over."

By the sounds of it, crickets currently ruled the equipment. The peaceful melody made the perfect accompaniment to Gabby's gentle company. Her care for her daughter inspired him to respond to Isabella in healthier ways. If this talk of travel was serious, perhaps he inspired her too.

Perhaps he could inspire her now to have a little fun.

He redirected their path across the spongy playground tiles to the swings.

She released his hand to grip the plastic-covered chain supporting the rubber seat. "I haven't done this in years. Years and years."

"Me neither, but why should the kids have all the fun?" He claimed his own swing and picked up his feet to swoop forward.

"Do you think they *are* having fun?" Gabby's question breezed by him as she set her own swing into motion, two seconds behind his. "Our girls?"

"I think they're trying to."

She swung backward, her hair brushed forward by the motion. "By their ages, I was married and planning a family and a career. So much more settled."

Tim couldn't claim the same. "They say people are getting married later and later in life."

Gabby peeked at him around the chain of her swing. "Are they now?"

He'd meant first marriages, but no matter. "That's the rumor. And I'm all for it."

Too forward?

Gabby's rich laugh reassured him, and a few more beats passed. "Am I terrible to consider leaving with everything going on with Charity?"

"You have a right to your own life." And he was ninety-nine percent sure he wasn't supporting independence because he wanted Gabby close. Wanted to converse with her daily, hold her hand, treat her to ridiculous dates. If only he could reach out, stop her swing, and kiss her.

Focusing, he inhaled for an entire forward trajectory and let the breath out as the swing dipped backward. "It may be time we step back and stop trying to orchestrate things for them. That's what I had to decide with Isabella. I flew her fiancé in. Since I'm never going to talk her out of him, and I'd rather not lose her over it."

Gabby matched her trajectory with his. "I'm scared that if I step back, I'll lose Charity."

"Our daughters have tolerated us so far. I don't think they'll suddenly shut us out if we give them what they've been asking for." Tim's phone buzzed two short beats. "Besides, allowing them more autonomy opens up more possibilities for us to pursue the lives we want."

"Like traveling."

"Exactly."

Though he hated to interrupt this, he had vowed to do better with Isabella. Ignoring her wouldn't do. He checked, but it was Lars who had texted. *Couldn't find her at The Depot, so I tried the address you sent. No one's answering.*

Tim texted him the code for the keyless lock on the front door. *Make yourself at home. Give me twenty minutes, and I'll see what I can find out.* Probably nothing, but once he'd talked with Gabby, he'd try anyway. He put the phone away and refocused.

The possibility of Gabby coming to California had flooded him with hope. But she hadn't been the one to name or praise the location. He didn't want to back off orchestrating things with Isabella only to pressure Gabby into a plan she didn't want.

"Were you thinking of California before I mentioned it?"

"I saw a position in Orange." She dragged her foot. "If I hadn't, I don't think I would've entertained the idea."

"Why not?"

She shifted her swing toward him long enough to study him, then let it fall back into place, facing forward. "Because it's too soon."

"To live near each other temporarily? Isn't that what we're doing now?"

She chuckled. "Fair point."

His phone vibrated again. Another message from Lars. He'd asked for twenty minutes, and it hadn't been five. He wouldn't sideline Gabby again so soon. "You've wanted to travel for years, and this way you'd have a friend nearby. We wouldn't have to instantly make our relationship serious. We could keep getting to know each other at our own pace."

"I'm afraid that if we got serious, I'd settle down in the first place I tried. Again."

Tim tipped his head, then pushed off and resumed swinging. "Only if you wanted. I'm portable."

"But you couldn't relocate for months at a time."

"I have. It's the internet age." He dragged his foot, slowing his motion to a sway. "But no matter where I call home, my job puts me on the road a week or two each month. Signing an unestablished artist would increase that." He twisted his swing toward her. "Would that be a dealbreaker?"

"I've been single a long time. I'm not afraid of time alone."

Gabby toed the ground, rocking. "But am I being impractical? How often do women pack up and set out on their own at fifty? That's something people do at twenty."

And playgrounds usually attracted five-year-olds. Still, he gripped the closer chain on her swing, syncing their movements. "Not everyone's free at fifty."

She let out a shaky sigh. "What if I regret it when I go?"

"Then you come back."

Gabby's face angled toward her feet. "They pay for housing wherever I go, so I can keep my house here—it's paid off, anyway—but my practice might be gone."

"You're highly employable. There must be other clinics around."

"Another job might not be at the same level or offer the cushy, Monday through Friday, nine to five hours. But ..." The chains creaked as she lifted her head. Moonlight glowed on the angles of her face as she studied the sky. "You're right. It's been a long-held dream—a long-forgotten one. When the girls suggested celebrating my fiftieth, a wind of change picked up, moving a few grains of sand at a time, and now the landscape is totally different. I don't know if it's my own doing or God's. I sort of think it's God's. But I don't want to walk away from responsibilities He has for me here."

"Isn't wind one way the Bible talks about the Holy Spirit? 'The wind has a mind of its own' ... or something." The Tim Paraphrase Version of the Bible probably wasn't even close.

"Huh." Gabby was silent for a beat. "It's in John. 'The wind blows where it wishes.' I hadn't thought of that." She took out her phone. A moment later, another thoughtful grunt escaped her lips. "The same verse says, 'you hear its sound, but you do not know where it comes from or where it goes. So it is with everyone who is born of the Spirit.'" She spoke with awe, so she must've teased some meaning out of the text.

Tim was out of his depth. And swings weren't nearly as

comfortable as they'd once been. He stood. "What do you think that means?"

"That God's on the move, and He doesn't want us to stagnate either." She rose, put her phone back in her pocket, then wrapped her arm in the chain, holding it securely enough to lean against. "I've let fear keep me here. Fear of losing Charity. Fear of the unknown. Of making a life in a new place." Her words churned out low and slow, as though she wasn't sure she wanted to see where they'd lead.

"It wouldn't be for the faint of heart." He stepped closer and took her free hand. "But you aren't faint of heart. I knew that from the moment I saw you."

She glanced up, flattered curiosity flashing in her eyes. "And I knew you were an adventure waiting to happen."

He grinned. He couldn't guess what had given her that idea, but knowing she craved adventure, he couldn't think of a bigger compliment. He chuckled, remembering his question from earlier. "Why should the kids have all the fun?"

"Because we're supposed to be the sensible ones? The voices of reason?"

"Life is short." He brushed her hair from her cheek. His phone went off a third time. Checking it would ruin the gossamer threads suspending the moment. He'd reply in five minutes. Surely whatever it was could wait that long. "The only *reasonable* course of action is to make the most of the opportunities God gives us."

He ran his thumb over her cheek, and her eyes sank closed. Leaning into the touch, she tilted her face to him. He dipped his head, and she lifted her lips to his for a soft, warm kiss. She pulled back and studied him. He might've apologized and stepped away but for the upturns at the corners of her mouth.

Her hand found his waist. "Is this one of those opportunities?"

The impulse to pull her even closer tensed his arms and

shoulders. He rested his hand along her neck, his fingertips in her hair, his thumb on her earlobe. Was the pulse tapping the base of his thumb hers or his own? "You tell me."

Her focus dipped to his mouth. His fingers traced her jaw forward, and when he touched her chin, she lifted it to meet his lips in a lingering kiss.

This was why love songs made so much money. No artist could capture the gift of such a moment, but bottle an ounce, and they'd be millionaires. Each movement was a give and take with a woman he respected. A picture of a life together unfolded before him. Dating. Traveling. A wedding. Mornings together ...

Even during his marriage, he'd failed to navigate life with a partner. He hadn't adjusted his travel schedule for her, discussed matters of the heart, or opened up his life in any of the million ways couples—the successful ones—did, often on an hour-by-hour basis. But with Gabby? He envisioned it all.

When the kiss broke off, she tucked her forehead against his neck, her chest rising and falling. "You're right." Her shoulders pulsed with a laugh as she pulled back. "I'm glad we didn't let the kids have all the fun."

"But we have to go back in?"

She patted his cheek and stepped away. "Even I've heard your phone go off."

Guilty as charged. He checked the device as he and Gabby made their way back to the front entrance. Lars had first asked if Isabella had shown up at The Depot. The most recent message revealed Lars' plan to come back.

Tim scanned the parking lot. He spotted the roof of his own rental, still where he'd parked it in the second row, so Isabella hadn't stopped in and helped herself to it. He didn't know what kind of vehicle Lars was driving. Tim had better get inside and start asking after Isabella as he'd promised.

On the front of the building, strings of patio lights glowed between the overhang's support beams. An amorous couple occupied the bench where Tim had first expected to talk with Gabby. Even in the dim light, Isabella's blonde hair shone.

Tim's feet stuck to the pavement at the base of the stairs. His stomach churned with conflicting reflexes. Look away? But the man wore a dark shirt, not a red one. And no way scrawny Lars boasted biceps like the one that flexed as the man cupped her neck.

"Isabella?" A man's voice cut from behind him.

She pulled away, eyes and mouth wide. Her fingers combed her hair, as if straightening it would erase from anyone's mind that she'd just been in the arms of a man who wasn't her fiancé.

David.

Tim pivoted toward the voice. Lars's chest heaved. His lips parted and his chin bunched. He looked to Tim, as though for help, but he didn't manage to speak.

On the bench, David's body remained angled toward Isabella, his eyes beady and black in the dim light. Lines of interest formed on his forehead, but the tip of his chin and the neutral set of his mouth showed no horror at being caught with someone else's intended.

Isabella braced her hands on the wooden slats of the bench. She eyed Tim, then focused beyond him. "What are you doing here, Lars?" Despite her initial flustered appearance, her voice conveyed calm control.

Lars flung his hand toward David. "Who's this?"

"None of your business."

David's arm shifted, and he rested his hand on Isabella's shoulder.

Lars vaulted the steps two at a time. Was there about to be a fight? Tim braced to race up after him, but David remained still, unthreatened.

Lars stopped near the door, a few feet off. "I heard you missed me." An angry tremor shook his words.

He didn't mention Tim, but Isabella's face shifted in his direction. "No, actually." She pursed her lips, then refocused on her fiancé.

He and Isabella had disagreed often, but he'd never been this horrified by the person she'd grown into.

"Then why'd your dad tell me to come?"

"Why did you listen to him?"

Lars offered no reply.

Tim took a breath and parted his lips. What could he say? What was happening?

Before he composed a satisfying answer, Isabella took David's hand and led him inside. He bumped Lars's shoulder on his way past, and the actor jerked back a step.

As the door shut behind them, Lars pivoted. Tim would've predicted self-righteous anger ... rage, even. Instead, Lars's shoulders fell.

Had Isabella and Lars agreed to an open relationship? They weren't on a break. Not with the way she'd argued for the relationship.

Lars descended the steps.

Tim debated moving closer, but with a situation this unpredictable, who knew what he'd be setting himself up for. He stayed put. "What was that?"

Lars scoffed. "You didn't know she dumped me?"

"She's been defending you. Wearing the ring."

"The one I gave her is back in New York. We went to an audition. I got a part, she didn't. She says I messed her up, but I wasn't anywhere near her when she tripped. What *is* my fault? Believing she was ready to take responsibility for her own two feet." He stormed off into the sea of cars.

Warmth on his arm reminded him of Gabby's presence. She was rubbing his forearm, lending comfort and reassurance. Tim scratched his head and peered toward the building. Should he talk to Isabella and get the rest of the story?

A car engine started. Where would Lars go? Straight back to the airport?

"By now, I should've learned not to surprise people."

"There's no way this happens a lot." Wry humor lifted Gabby's voice.

"Depends on what you mean by 'this.'" The men of Awestruck could tell stories of Tim showing up unannounced, keeping secrets, and making arrangements for others without their involvement.

Some surprises had worked out. Others he'd rather forget. Bringing Lars to Many Oaks had crashed like an asteroid into the second camp.

12

———

Mid-day sun glared down on Gabby as she stopped about twenty feet from the picnic table outside Charity's work. In the shade of a maple tree, her daughter chatted with co-workers, enjoying a break. As she waited for Charity to notice her, she wondered how Esther must've felt, waiting for the king to raise his scepter or condemn her to death.

Charity offered the mercy of a small smile. She excused herself from her friends and approached, hands tucked away, expression cautious.

"I come in peace." As Gabby said it, the line seemed like overkill.

Charity didn't call her on it.

Gabby surveyed the bench, the people, and the clinic across the way where she had worked since before Charity's birth. Remembering her pregnancy, she rubbed the small of her back.

Was she ready to abandon that former self for a new adventure? At the thought of last evening with Tim, eagerness welled in her chest and threatened to spill out in a giggle. She hadn't been kissed like that since Judah. Even that had been different, because in their marriage, a passionate kiss tended to lead to other things. She'd forgotten the pleasure of kissing for its own sake with a man who admired and protected her.

Her new adventure promised more time with him, a warmer climate, and an unfamiliar area to explore. For those adventures, she was ready. But could she cope with the distance from Charity? It hadn't stirred up such melancholy when Natalie had left Many Oaks, but looking back, perhaps Gabby had become more overbearing with Charity afterward, transferring her mothering from two daughters to the remaining one.

"Is everything okay?" Concern shaded Charity's eyes.

A full-grown woman, she'd take the skills Gabby and Judah had instilled in her and use them for her own purposes. Gabby could either allow that or fight a losing battle to control her.

Lord, please woo her soul.

He was in control, after all, and only He could capture Charity's heart and steer her toward ultimate good. It had never been Gabby's job.

Despite that knowledge, the announcement she'd come to make—that she planned to leave Many Oaks—caught in her throat.

"Let's walk for a minute."

Charity checked her phone then nodded, perhaps keeping an eye on the time. A responsible act. Gabby could take comfort in that. And many other things.

They started down the sidewalk.

"I'm sorry for not hearing you when you told me what you thought and what you wanted."

Charity's gaze dipped to her feet. "I didn't say much. I didn't mean to surprise you about Reese. I wanted to ease into telling you."

Any plan that didn't involve letting Gabby know in advance

of the move sounded faulty, but Gabby held her peace. She'd promised she would, after all. "You're an adult, and I've raised you the best I could. I make mistakes, but I'm very proud of the intelligent, beautiful woman you've become. You're ready to make your own way in the world, and I didn't mean to muddle your transition into independence."

"You didn't, Mom. It's fine. You're a great mom."

"Growing up means sorting through the good and bad of your childhood and your relationship with your parents and deciding who you'll be and how you'll live. You're on your way with that—and rightfully so."

Charity squinted, suspicion playing across her face. "Where is this coming from?"

Trees, buildings, and powerlines stood between them and the horizon. A familiar feeling of being boxed in pressed on her chest. "I've always wanted to travel more."

"You must get tons of vacation time. You've had the same job forever."

She did have over a month each year, but the time wouldn't cover even one locum tenens position. "Your father and I used to dream of moving around every few years. We never followed through, but I can now."

She paused. How she wished this could've gone to plan, that she could've made this announcement after she was more comfortable with Charity's direction in life.

The Lord hadn't granted that, however. Instead, through her conversation with Tim the night before and prayer and journaling that morning, He'd granted assurances that the time had come to follow His prompting regardless.

With a deep breath, she plunged ahead. "I'm going to become a travel nurse practitioner. They take contracts to work in a place for three to six months. I'm thinking of starting in California."

Charity stopped walking. "California?"

Gabby faced her. "Obtaining the necessary license will be a slow process—it'll take months. I wanted to give you as much warning as possible so you're not taken by surprise."

"Like I surprised you?" Charity's back straightened. "Is this a punishment? You're mad because I let Reese move in and didn't tell you."

"I can't say that didn't hurt, but"—Gabby touched her arm—"this is something I'm doing for me because I think God is leading me this way."

"California." This time, accusation rang in her tone. "Where Tim lives. Because God wants you there."

"I don't know what God has in mind for him and me. I do hope to find a position near LA. We enjoy each other's company. We're not serious yet, but we could be, in time."

Charity scoffed. "How much time he has is up for debate. You know that, right?"

How was she supposed to answer? Life had taught her the uncertainty of tomorrow in a general sense. However, Charity seemed to have a specific threat in mind.

"He has a tumor in his pancreas. Those are bad, aren't they?"

A falling sensation swooped through her stomach, but she straightened her spine, resisting the rollercoaster of assumptions. "Do you know any details?"

"Only that Isabella is afraid he's dying."

She and Tim had met on Monday. Would he have told her if he had a serious health issue? Perhaps not, when they only had one week together, but once she'd started talking about spending a few months in California, he should've told her. Unless he was still uncertain of his diagnosis. Some benign tumors required nothing more than monitoring, but not all tumors were benign.

"All this talk about my childhood ..." Charity's eyes glazed over, years gone by presumably playing in her mind. "The only problem was losing Dad. And don't claim that didn't wreck you too. I don't want to see you go through that again."

Gabby certainly didn't want to. As she pushed her hands back in her pockets, they trembled against her leg. "I appreciate you looking out for me."

"You'll stay away from him?"

"I'll *talk* to him." Gabby waited for the statement to land before nudging Charity back toward her office. Though desperate to learn details, she had patients until she would have to leave to meet Natalie's flight. She could call while driving to the airport, but she'd rather not have such a serious conversation behind the wheel. Tomorrow at lunch would have to do.

Charity's posture remained rigid. "You can't just run away and leave it all behind, Mom. Especially not over someone you just met this week."

"I'm not leaving because of Tim. I've wanted to travel for a long time."

"You can't go, Mom." Charity's voice held the same ache Gabby had felt when Charity spoke of her loss of faith.

Gabby's certainty wobbled, but remembering the peace she'd felt this morning as she'd spent time with God, she put an arm around her daughter's still-stiff shoulders. "Who knows, sweetie. The Lord might lead in a way I don't expect, but for now, I think this is the right thing for me to pursue. Change is hard, but we each have a responsibility for our own lives. The blessing in this is we get to be friends now."

"How can we be friends? You don't even like me."

Gabby pulled her stiff form into a hug. "I *love* you."

"You weren't supposed to take Reese moving in so hard. I'll ask him to leave."

Charity still thought this was about her living arrangements? But in the statement, Gabby recognized Charity's attempt to control her. Not that Gabby could blame her. Gabby herself had wanted to stay in Many Oaks so she'd have more sway over Charity. Recognizing her flawed desire to control her adult daughter had been a big part of how she'd come to terms with the plan to leave.

"I'd love it if you did, but unless it's a choice you make for yourself, you'll just resent me." Besides, what Gabby really wanted for Charity was a heart change, not an outward show. That level of transformation depended on God, not Gabby. "Let's do each other the favor of not trying to control each other, even when we disagree. No matter where I travel, you can always call. I'm still your mom. I'll always love you." She released the hug Charity had never relaxed into anyway and patted her daughter's cheek. "And if you ever change your mind, all you have to do is ask, and you'll find your Heavenly Father ready to connect with you too."

"Mom." Charity tucked her hands in her pockets. "It's you I'm worried about."

Gabby rubbed her daughter's arms and stepped back. "I'm going to be okay. You are too. So are we."

She spoke in faith, not in herself or the power of human love, but in God's goodness.

Except God sometimes allowed hard, hard things. Things like Charity denying the faith, Judah dying, and illness. If she and Tim became serious for the long haul, she'd expect hardship balanced by many good years. But for it to come so soon? Right at the start?

She wanted adventure and love. Not heartache.

After Judah had died, Aunt Gladys had hugged her fiercely and said, "Honey, God's holding you in this."

He had carried her through, but it'd been a bumpy ride, and she wasn't ready to go through it again.

"WHY IS THIS A PROBLEM?" Tim stood in the doorway of Isabella's room as she tucked the last of her belongings in her suitcase.

"Because it's always something with you." She dropped the flap and tugged the zipper.

"Last night, it was something with *you*." When he'd approached Isabella during the show, she'd brushed him off. After Blaze wrapped up, he and Gabby had called it a night. Back at the rental, Tim waited up for Isabella until the bars closed. She hadn't materialized until an hour later, after he was in bed.

This morning, she'd holed up in her room until noon, only to emerge bent on packing up and leaving. Gabby must've shared her travel plans with Charity, because Charity had passed the news to Isabella. But why did Isabella care? Her anger must trace back to Lars instead.

Tim scratched his unshaven jaw. "If you'd told me you'd broken up, I wouldn't have invited him here."

"You want to discuss news we haven't told each other?"

"I came clean about my diagnosis, and I would've told you about the possibility of Gabby coming to California except you weren't speaking to me. Yesterday was the first I heard of it. It wasn't a secret. But you? Wearing a ring and failing to tell me you'd broken up with your fiancé? How many times have we talked about him on this trip?"

Isabella stabbed a fist against her hip. "How often did we talk about your health?"

Because he'd been avoiding the subject, they hadn't, aside from Isabella's occasional comments. *"You're lucky you're dying."*

Since God worked all things for good, was it a blessing life as they knew it didn't go forever? There was something in Genesis, that book he'd read each time he'd reattempted a read-through, about God keeping Adam and Eve from the tree of life so they wouldn't live forever in their fallen state. Was death tied to redemption?

Apparently interpreting his pause as an admission, Isabella nodded once. "Exactly." She hefted the suitcase off the bed and rolled it through the house. She stopped beside the door, her profile visible to Tim. Her fingers flew across the face of her phone for the third time since she'd gone on this rampage. Arranging a ride, he assumed, since he hadn't volunteered.

"Issy, why didn't you tell me?"

Her lips tightened as if she were about to spit out an insult. "Is-a-*bell*-a. If you didn't want to deal with four syllables, you shouldn't have given them to me."

The name had been her mother's choice. Tim had lobbied for something sweet and simple. Amy or Julie or Emma. Short and sweet. His negotiation skills had failed then for the same reason they faltered now—"no" hath no ally like a woman scorned.

But why was she so very hurt?

"I don't understand what's going on with you. Since lunch yesterday—"

"—when you told me you'd been deceiving me for *weeks*—"

"Just like you were deceiving me." He lifted his eyebrows in accusation.

With a frustrated groan, she checked her phone again. "Finally." She yanked open the door and thumped her bag over the threshold.

A slick black sedan waited at the curb. David circled the hood, on course to help Isabella with her luggage.

"Where are you going?" Tim advanced down the walk, unsure what he'd do when he reached her. Restraining her was out of the question, but barring that, he'd never get her to stay.

With both hands, she lifted the suitcase over the grass between the sidewalk and road. "To the airport."

Tim crossed his arms. He hated to see her struggling, but he wasn't about to help her leave. "And then?"

David opened the back door of the car, and Isabella braced the suitcase with her knee as she tugged it upward. The bulky load caught on the seat. David took over, sliding the bag onto the seat before stepping back to open the front passenger's door for Isabella.

"All good things come to an end, Dad, and I realized a long time ago that it's easier when I do the ending." She slung her purse in, then dropped into the seat.

"That's what happened with Lars? You broke it off because you were afraid he was going to?"

"Eventually. Everybody's got to look out for themselves. It's just how it is."

"No. It's how it was for you because of me. But I'm trying to prove life can work differently. You don't have to push people away to protect yourself. You don't have to push me away."

"No push required. You wander off anytime you see a good musician or a pretty, single woman."

"You're leaving, not me."

"I leave first. Hurts less this way." She yanked the door. "Don't follow me."

His arms burned to pull the handle and continue the conversation, but David steered away from the curb. Tim watched until the vehicle turned out of sight, rubbing his chest as the sharp barbs of failure lodged in his heart.

13

At least someone still enjoyed seeing him. When Tim arrived at the café for lunch, Gabby greeted him with a kiss on the cheek, a gesture he returned. Her now-familiar perfume hinted at apples and flowers.

Gabby flashed an uncertain smile as she stepped back.

Had he lingered too long? Or could she tell he was in a low mood over Isabella? He didn't want his falling out with his daughter the day before to ruin this lunch too. He took a seat at the table where she'd been seated. "What's good here?"

"Their roasted vegetable panini is amazing." She set her menu aside.

The possibility of cancer had inspired an instant diet change, and he'd lost weight that had been creeping up on him. While he was grateful to look his best for Gabby, even he had his limits. "What do you suggest for the carnivores among us?"

Her cheeks rounded. "You can't go wrong. This place does an amazing job."

Settled on a roast beef sandwich, he stacked his menu on Gabby's. He should update her about Isabella. If only pushing his daughter away didn't prove what a failure he was. Gabby might take it personally, given Isabella had high-tailed it as soon as she found out about Gabby coming to California. "So you picked up Natalie last night?"

Gabby nodded. "Somehow, she's more polished every time I see her. She seems happy."

"That's great. What does she do?"

"She's director of e-commerce for Estelle Cosmetics."

Tim's working knowledge of cosmetics was non-existent, but not many people so young held director roles. "Impressive."

"We stayed up way too late catching up. Charity took today off to spend time with her. Uncharacteristic, but ..." Gabby poked her straw around in her water, rattling ice cubes. "Well, I think Natalie relates to her better than I do. She might help Charity move in the right direction."

The girls would be prepping for tonight's party. Tim prayed Gabby's hopes would come true. The waiter took their orders, and as he left, leaden reluctance replaced Tim's hunger.

Gabby leaned her elbow on the table and rubbed her neck. "You know small towns are famous for rumors."

She'd already heard? The heaviness in his stomach dissipated. "Isabella thinks she's safer if she ends things at the first sign of a threat."

Gabby squinted. "That's what happened with Lars?"

"And with me."

She tilted her head in confusion.

Were they not talking about the same thing? What other rumor could she have meant? "She left yesterday. You heard?"

"No. I'm sorry. What threat worried her so much?"

Whatever topic she'd meant to introduce, they'd have to finish this one first. He took a deep breath, but the tension in his chest returned as he exhaled. "My divided attention."

"Divided by me?"

"And Blaze and Million Dollar Ransom. Though the problems started before we left LA. We both kept some key facts to ourselves for too long. In the past, I would've given up, too. Cut the trip short. But not this time." He let his cheeks puff up and exhaled a long sigh. "She's wrong though. I doubt she's hurting any less than I am."

"I'm sure." After a loaded beat, she offered a sad smile. "I'm sorry our plans were part of the problem. Charity has concerns too. She thinks I'm trying to punish her for letting Reese move in."

Tim winced. "And Natalie?"

"She moved away years ago. She's all for it. Says I deserve to be happy."

"You do."

The comment didn't dislodge her sadness, reminding Tim she'd tried to bring up something else. Something that apparently concerned her more than Isabella. What could be worse? Something with one of her girls? Something between him and her?

He fought for a relaxed tone. "You mentioned small towns being famous for gossip. If it wasn't about Isabella, what did you hear?"

"That you're sick."

To her ears, Gabby's voice croaked out the news that had been stabbing at her peace of mind since Charity had shared it yesterday. Maybe, to put herself back at ease, she should've done this over the phone between patients yesterday. Ripped the bandage off.

"Oh." Tim sat back in his chair, his grimace showing his bottom teeth. Confusion didn't furrow his forehead, so he knew what she was talking about.

This wasn't a surprise. At least, not to him.

Her hunger pangs muted, chewing on dread.

"Isabella said something?" he asked.

"Yes, to Charity." And Gabby had refused to jump to conclusions. Leaping into despair a few words into the conversation would serve no one well. "Indirectly. She told Charity she was worried about your health because of a pancreatic tumor."

"Intraductal papillary mucinous neoplasm." He enunciated each word, as though he'd memorized the sounds without comprehending the meaning. "It showed up on abdominal scans after a car accident. I'm symptom-free, but I hunted down a nationally recognized specialist, and he did a biopsy. It's not cancer yet, but depending on when Isabella talked to Charity, she may not have known that last part until later."

"Not cancer yet?" Even as she repeated the good news, her heart thumped like a scared rabbit's.

"It's pre-cancerous, so they're taking it out." His lips tightened. "They're taking the tumor, that is, not my whole pancreas. Laparoscopic distal pancreatomy. Six-to-eight-week recovery time, but that should take care of it."

More good news. A Whipple procedure to remove the whole organ carried far more risk. So why did her muscles feel as flimsy as paper? "When will they operate?"

"Late October. I should be back to normal by Christmas." He adjusted his napkin on the table. "You know, I ..." He scratched his head. "I'm not always the best at sharing updates at the right times. I wanted to bring it up as soon as you mentioned you worked in healthcare, but I didn't want to dump it on you. Until the night before last, when we started talking about you coming to California, it didn't have much bearing on this." He motioned between them. "At least, I thought it didn't." He bit his lip and fell silent.

Could she fault him for keeping mum? They'd only known each other a few days. Yet here she sat, flattened by the surprise into something akin to a paper doll controlled by someone else. She heard herself offer a counterpoint. "Obtaining what I'll need to practice in California and finding the right position could take a few months."

He groaned. "You might move while I'm laid up from the operation. I'm sorry. That's relevant. I should've mentioned it."

A reasonable person would reassure him. Once again her mouth and brain bypassed her turmoil. "Orange must be at least an hour from you, and who knows if I'll end up there. Wherever I work, I suppose we'd mostly see each other on weekends."

"After the operation, I won't be able to meet you partway or come to you for a few weeks. I doubt I'll get out much at all."

"People have surgery. It's a fact of life. A benefit of living in this day and age, actually." She breathed deeply to crowd out the panic her lungs soaked up like sponges.

Tim's blue eyes remained fixed on her like he knew there was more she wasn't saying.

And there was, but she didn't understand her anxiety herself, let alone have the words to share it with someone else.

The waiter approached with a tray. He paused before setting the first plate. "Vegetable panini?"

Frozen, she didn't even think to indicate herself.

Tim pointed for her, and the waiter doled out the meals.

"Can I get you anything else?"

Security. Assurances. As the words rose through the murky waters of her mind, her nose tingled. Was it turning pink?

Tim took one look at her, then said to the waiter, "We're good. Thanks."

Good? Gabby rubbed her neck.

She'd had twenty-four hours to acclimate to the idea of Tim having a tumor. She'd hoped his condition wouldn't require treatment, but this was manageable. More than manageable.

Yet she wasn't good.

Even a healthy person couldn't promise tomorrow, let alone months or years of health and happiness. She'd lost middle-aged patients to all manner of diseases. Then there were the sudden tragedies. Drownings. Falls. Car wrecks. Like Judah's.

"Gabby?" Tim's hand covered hers. "If this changes where you want to work, that's okay."

Her rigid neck barely allowed her to shake her head. The operation wouldn't have a significant impact on their relationship. She liked the idea of talking him through recovery while being close enough to check on him in person over the weekends. Her skills could prove helpful.

The desire to lend comfort was part of what scared her. They hadn't known each other long, and yet they'd bonded over their struggles with their daughters, their appreciation of travel, their similar values. It'd happened as fast as a riptide, but she hadn't yet been pulled out to sea. She could escape the current, swim back to the shore of a life lived without romance. After all, loving and losing again just might drown her. It nearly had the first time.

"If I'd known this was a deal breaker for you, I would've told you sooner. I never meant to mislead you."

"You didn't. No." She rested her wrists on the edge of the table, hand poised to pick up the sandwich she wasn't sure she could stomach. "Needing surgery isn't a deal breaker."

"Then what is?"

Dying. The potential to die. The eventuality of death. Why had a treatable issue dredged up all these fears? If she and Tim did get serious and each lived normal life expectancies, they would have more years together than she and Judah had enjoyed. Any loss would be decades in the future, Lord willing.

She'd thought she'd stayed single because no one had interested her. What if, instead, she'd isolated herself from the possibility of becoming a widow twice over?

How did people do this again after the pain of the first time?

Tim's eyes swam with concern.

She gulped, blinked, worked on breathing. "I think

arranging a move and talking about surgery made it all seem very serious very quickly."

"If you want to keep your options open, see other people, that's ... okay."

She shook her head. "I'm not interested in anyone else either."

"Either?" The serious set of his face suggested he knew her meaning.

The word had slipped out. She didn't want to see him or anyone else because she preferred to avoid loss. But was that true? Did she wish to distance herself from him over fear?

Her head said to collect herself. Enjoy the first man she'd been attracted to in a decade. Her heart, however, banged in her chest like a prisoner desperate to escape an executioner.

"What about taking a different assignment, then reconsidering the Los Angeles area afterward?" he suggested. "A few months would give me time to get healthy and our relationship, if that's what we decide we want, time to breathe."

She nodded faintly, then with more intention. "I'll think about it. I'm ..." Should she even share this?

The crease between his brows and the anxious slant of his eyes told her she'd better.

"I'm realizing I have some old trauma that's not as healed as I thought."

The crease deepened.

"Losing Judah was hard."

"My prognosis is great. Ninety-five percent of people do fine."

"It's not that. It's, um ... loving and losing. Not from this. Just in general." With a cringe, she fell silent to see if he'd make sense of her rambling, because she didn't seem capable of doing any better.

"You lost him unexpectedly, and me having a health concern reminded you of the frailty of life." He'd hit the issue so squarely on the head, her eyes watered. Compassion tipped his mouth as he exhaled and squeezed her hand. "That's understandable."

She was so surprised by his reaction that she laughed. "It is? Because I'm in the doghouse with myself right now."

"I came to Christ because someone I care about had a close call. If *almost* losing a friend changed me, burying a spouse must have lifelong repercussions."

"I suppose it does." She eyed the door, but they hadn't touched their food yet. Tim hadn't caused any of this, and whatever she decided long term, she didn't want to cause a scene so close to the end of his stay in Many Oaks. Her fingers shook as she slid them under her now-cool panini.

Tim changed the subject and carried the conversation as she choked down half of her sandwich and coleslaw. Even as they said goodbye, he didn't ask for her thoughts on their relationship or California. Perhaps he sensed she couldn't make promises regarding their future because God wouldn't either.

If trauma from her last venture into love still haunted her, how could she sign up for more?

14

"You're not planning to put a bag over my head, are you?" The grief that had lapped at Gabby since lunch ebbed, thanks to her daughters' antics. She pinched her keys and held them mid-air between herself and her eldest.

Charity intercepted.

Natalie brandished a black cloth from a pocket hidden in the folds of her dress. "It's a blindfold."

"We're classy kidnappers." Charity wiggled her eyebrows and motioned Gabby to turn.

Gabby's low heels clicked against her tile entryway as she pivoted. Only one restaurant in town, Meliore's, was nice enough to warrant the outfit her daughters had insisted she wear. The navy-blue A-line dress flattered her figure by tapering at the narrowest part of her waist, then swishing to her knees. At her neck, the same diamond pendant she'd worn to her wedding glittered in its lovely, understated way.

She rubbed the pendant.

Judah.

Dwelling on him would drag her back into the depths. She

moved her fingers up and back, brushing her flashy costume earrings. Though she hadn't felt like celebrating as she'd chosen the jewelry, she'd determined to look the part of a happy birthday girl in hopes that her feelings would follow.

As Natalie positioned the blindfold, Charity popped around front to ensure correct placement. They hadn't had the opportunity to revisit her travel plans or Tim's prognosis, and Gabby was in no rush. Overcome with grief and worry, what would she say? She couldn't imagine going to California anymore. Should she leave Many Oaks at all?

The blindfold replaced Charity's playful smile. If her daughter put conflicts aside for a night, Gabby ought to follow suit. Natalie put an arm around her back and gripped her hand. Charity flanked her other side.

Their awkward progress had them all, Gabby included, giggling by the time they reached the car.

This felt good. The laughter. Natalie's presence. A truce with Charity. A celebration to dress up for. When she'd thought about her fiftieth birthday in years past, she hadn't realized how young she'd feel. How much like herself. The same self she'd been all this time.

The car hummed, accelerating more than a drive into the heart of Many Oaks would allow.

They might've planned dinner in some other town. "How long am I stuck wearing this blindfold?"

"Couple more minutes." Natalie braked again. The blinker sounded, and the car pulled to the right.

After several other accelerations and righthand turns, Gabby suspected they'd gone in circles meant to disorient her. And perhaps it had worked. When the vehicle pulled to a stop, she could've sworn they weren't at Meliore's.

"Hang tight." Natalie's car door sounded.

The armrest pulled away from Gabby's elbow as one of her

daughters came for her. Before getting out, she reached for the blindfold. "I can take this off, right?"

"Not yet." Charity's voice accompanied a guiding hand on her arm. "We'll let you know."

A distant voice called out to someone. The hum of passing traffic seemed too far off and too fast for Meliore's. Instead of garlic, the savory scent of fried food floated on the air.

She placed her feet as carefully as she would if she were walking on thin ice. "You want me to walk into ... whatever this is blindfolded?"

"You're the one who wanted more adventure." Charity's tone warned her to be careful what she wished for.

If only her daughter had granted other wishes instead of testing this one. "I still like to know where I'm going."

An arm interlocked with hers, opposite Charity. Natalie's voice came light and teasing. "It wouldn't be an adventure if you knew what was coming."

Gabby halted. Was that true? And did God mean for her to apply it beyond tonight to her future with Tim?

The girls pressed her onward. Reflection would have to wait.

"I'd feel a lot more comfortable with a heads-up. For all I know, I'm about to walk off a cliff."

Charity jostled her arm. "You think we'd do that to you?"

She continued this time, but she felt the Lord echoing the question. Did Gabby really believe He'd set her up for senseless loss and pain? No. He had purpose, even in the difficulty.

"It's the exact opposite." Amusement tinged Natalie's reply. "You're in front of a set of five stairs. Step up. We won't let you fall."

Just like her Lord. Sometime after this blindfold came off, she'd have to find the courage to live like it. She scrunched her nose against an itch. "I know we're at The Depot." The location had five stairs and matched the sounds and aroma. "Can I take the blindfold off?"

"Nope. Up you go."

She kicked two steps on the way up, but her daughters steadied her. They'd either proceeded with a surprise party or decorated a table they didn't want her to see. The party seemed more likely.

"We're going inside. Stepping over the threshold." The slight rise didn't normally cause issues, but blindfolded, she was grateful for Charity's narration.

They would be in the dining room now. Patrons must be getting a kick out of this.

By her estimation, they advanced to the event hall. Surprise party it was.

She swallowed a complaint about her daughters ignoring her wishes. Even with the blindfold in place—perhaps especially because of the blindfold—she could tell they'd gone to a lot of trouble.

Something soft and papery brushed her shoulder. A streamer? Glasses clinked back and to her right, where she guessed the bar was. Savory aromas—bacon, burgers, sauteed onions, and deep-fried offerings—melded in the air. Ahead of her stretched a quiet, black cavern. Probably filled with party-goers awaiting the cue to shout. Picturing them smiling and fidgeting, as she'd done when she'd been part of a surprise party, Gabby herself started to smile.

Natalie—Gabby guessed since her left arm had been released—started on the blindfold knot. As the fabric dropped away, two competing choruses rose.

"Surprise!"

"Happy birthday!"

Her eyes struggled to adjust. Beyond tables with white linens stood a dozen guests. Wait. A crowd stood behind the first row. Fifty? Sixty people? Gabby flattened a hand against her breastbone. Fifty or sixty friends had come to surprise her?

Natalie was right. Ignorance made the reveal more thrilling. She would've tried to stop all this if she'd known it was coming, but what a blessing to see love and joy shining in so many familiar faces.

What surprises might God have in store, if she allowed Him to lead her?

Charity squeezed her in a hug. Her satiny dress felt smooth and warm as Gabby rubbed her back in a silent thank you. "I know you said no party, but we couldn't resist. We love you so much." She bit her lip as she stepped back, her expression a plea for Gabby's praise.

If she could speak, she'd give it. Gabby touched her mouth as she took in more details. White linens covered the tables, and centerpieces of votives and floral arrangements adorned them. A two-tiered cake stood off to one side, gifts and cards crowded around it. On the other side of the room, buffet tables held steaming food.

But the people were the touching part. Anson stood beside Sydney. Nearby were three of the other Lions from Judah's final team, Cody, Samuel, and Sterling. Touching. She hadn't realized they cared enough to show up en force.

A fifth Lion, David, appeared to have captured the interest of a new woman. Oh, correction. That was his little sister, Marissa, beside him.

Others from work, the community, and church fanned out from there. Some she'd considered friends for years, some more acquaintances, yet they'd all come to celebrate her.

"Welcome, everyone." At the voice, the guests turned toward where Blaze stood at the microphone. "Happy birthday, Gabby!"

Gabby waved in response, but her attention slipped back to her guests. Look at them all!

The few who hadn't pivoted toward the stage stood out. A waiter added another vat of potatoes to the buffet. A couple of people whispered to each other. But only one person met her gaze.

While some of the other men looked stiff in ill-fitting button-downs, perhaps purchased years ago and never replaced, Tim's appeared tailored to his chest and arms. He had the cuffs rolled up to his elbows, and his brown leather belt accented his trim waist. Dark blue pants and brown shoes completed the look. She met his gaze and realized she'd checked him out from head to toe. Instead of smirking as he would've been justified to do, he returned her eye contact another moment before—reluctantly, it seemed—focusing on Blaze.

He wanted to know where they stood. He had every right to know.

Her heart thumped away. God had powerfully illustrated what He was calling her to. All that remained was for her to work up the gumption to act on it.

First Natalie, then Charity glanced her way. They hadn't sought her approval like this since they'd made her breakfast in bed as little girls. She squeezed their hands, hoping to impart her gratitude.

As soon as their attention shifted away, she stole another glance at Tim. His hair appeared gelled tonight. She longed to mess it up, but before attempting any such thing, she needed to right what had gone wrong at lunch.

God was good. She could trust Him, even in the unknown. With the repetition of the truth, her fears shrank. Within a few hours, the truth might subdue them completely. By then, the party would be breaking up, or at least quieting down. She would reconnect with Tim then and hope God was giving him a similar message of reassurance about her.

~

Tim found a seat at a table of strangers and set about asking questions to avoid having to answer many himself. After the meal, people filled out trivia about Gabby, prepared by her daughters. When Gabby revealed the answers, the winner would receive a gift card to The Depot.

Interest in Gabby, rather than the gift card, narrowed his focus to the paper. He tapped the butt of his pen on the table as he read.

What is Gabby's full name?

What is Gabby's favorite color?

Does Gabby prefer pizza or tacos?

Where did Gabby grow up?

Tim wouldn't win trivia tonight. He didn't know any of these.

A hand smoothed across his shoulders. "Gabrielle Lynn Voss." As the woman in question murmured the answer, her cheek brushed his ear. She claimed the seat a retired banker had occupied until a few minutes before.

Anticipation raced down his spine, but memories of lunch sent a fast and effective cease order. Gabby wasn't his, and she might never be. He didn't scrawl down the answer. One out of a dozen wouldn't get him anywhere. " I hope this was a good surprise."

Her eyes lit as she scanned the room. "I specifically asked *not* to have this. But I'm glad they ignored me." She winked at him, then her expression sobered. "I hear this is why we had lunch today."

"One reason, but not the important one."

Regret creased her eyes. "And then I went and—"

"Asked important questions. In return, you told the truth about how you were feeling."

She surveyed the room, then angled closer. "I meant to wait, but—"

"Well, if it isn't the birthday girl!" The booming voice signaled the return of the banker. He reached around Gabby to set his cake at his place.

She glanced at the slab of vanilla, then relinquished the seat to its original occupant. She reached as if to put her hand back on Tim's shoulder, but before she'd made contact, Charity hustled up.

"Time to go share the answers, Mom." She motioned Gabby toward the stage, where Blaze had just finished a song.

Gabby shot him an apologetic look.

He waved it off. "Enjoy your party. We'll talk later."

Charity herded her to the microphone.

He listened to her answers, surprised by some and not by others. Her favorite color was plum, the color of the shirt she'd worn when they'd attended Blaze's show on Monday. The day they'd met.

After one of the older ladies from the movie night won trivia, Gabby made the rounds. She glanced his way, as though intending to circle back. He gave a smile he hoped would convey she should take her time. They couldn't have much of a conversation here, and even if they tried, he doubted he'd like the outcome.

His attention wandered to a slideshow following Gabby from infancy to the present.

High school Gabby in a red cap and gown brandished a diploma. College Gabby in a dated pair of glasses poured over books. And there she was, beaming beside a rugged guy with a crooked grin who peered down at her with adoration.

Judah.

Jealousy skewered him. Gabby deserved love, a life partner, and the blessing of her daughters. He couldn't begrudge her that. But why should the guy get to keep her heart after he'd died?

The years advanced through their wedding, the move to Many Oaks, and the birth of their girls.

On and on. Posed pictures and candid ones. Some funny, some sweet.

Judah's disappearance from the timeline was sudden. The entire family smiled in a Christmas photo, the girls teenagers. But only Gabby posed with her daughters in their caps and gowns for their high school graduations.

A few minutes later, the Gabby on screen matched the one Tim knew.

Or wished he knew. He glanced down at the trivia paper. He'd objected to a whirlwind romance when the girls had suggested he spend time with Gabby, yet they'd run headlong into drastic plans. He'd minimized it, but he'd never proven himself capable of loving anyone well. Gabby could be out a job she loved if she tried traveling and wanted to come back home. Why surrender a sure thing for the gigantic question mark that was Tim?

Blaze crossed between him and the slideshow, met his eye, and started his way. She might've assumed he'd been watching her and not the projected images. He scooted back in his seat, sitting up straighter and ordering his thoughts.

Million Dollar Ransom might blow him away at tomorrow's show, but they couldn't have more talent than the artist who perched on the chair beside his. "I'm sorry I had to run out the other day. Normally, I have more flexibility, but a customer scheduled an appointment for help with features on their new car. All the little icons and options confuse people."

"No problem. Follow-through is important."

"Exactly. I don't want to be one of those pushy salespeople who disappears as soon as my commission's in the bank. So ..." She pulled her hair over her shoulder and tipped her head. "What advice do you have for me?"

Wow. Humble enough to lead by asking for feedback.

"What are your goals?"

She inhaled, a helpless frown on her lips. "Well." She blew out the breath. "I want to give the best performances I can." Her gaze roamed the room. "I like to give them a good show. It does something for my ego, you know?" With a self-deprecating laugh, she lowered her lashes. "Historically speaking, I've been known as something of a delinquent."

"You? No." Delinquents didn't build email lists, hustle up gigs, and take time to explain car features after the sale.

Blaze shrugged one shoulder. "Knowing they enjoy having me on stage a couple times a week and that Philip feels it's worthwhile to introduce me to his hotshot manager is a huge compliment."

If she was content with such scraps, she had no idea the magnitude of her talent. Perhaps living in proximity to Philip and Michaela, who'd both found fame and fortune in music, had skewed her perspective of the rarity of skills like hers. "You could go beyond all this."

"I'm flattered, but I couldn't do that to Mercy—my little sister. I have custody. She's been through a lot. Is going through a lot. Sometimes, prayer and routines are all that get us through the day."

"It takes a ..." The slideshow caught his eye. He'd been about to say raising a kid took a village, a segue into asking if another family member might care for Mercy while Blaze traveled. But the pictures touted family and community. Tim had failed to prioritize either, and his relationships had crumbled. He wouldn't persuade Blaze to embark on a journey that could result in similar brokenness. No amount of record sales or fame or royalties would justify leaving a little girl without her guardian.

He cleared his throat and started again. "It takes compassion and courage to put someone else first. She's blessed to have you."

As though again underestimating the rarity of her character, she shifted away from the compliment by rising. "Thank you. It was good meeting you."

Emotional breakthroughs had never been his forte. He asked God to break through where he couldn't hope to. "Take care, Blaze."

Once she'd gone, his attention drifted to Gabby. She directed her warm attention on an elderly couple, nodding as the woman spoke. A small line of people waited for her company.

Like Blaze, she had a life here. Family and community. Meanwhile, Isabella could never assemble a slideshow about him because he'd been absent. His daughter couldn't have answered these questions about Tim, and he'd struggle to answer some of them about her.

Yet he'd bet good money Charity and Natalie could've filled in answers for their dad, despite living without him for ten years. Judah had used the time he'd had wisely.

Tim couldn't say the same.

What he *could* say? He had no more business talking Gabby into leaving than he'd had convincing Blaze to go. The honorable option was to respect her reservations, bow out, and salvage what he could with Isabella. He had promised Gabby a conversation later, but later would have to be tomorrow. He wouldn't ruin her party or take her away from her guests by breaking the news tonight.

He pushed the blank trivia sheet toward the center of the table and left.

A FLARE of anxiety shot through Tim's chest when his phone went off. He'd left Isabella a voicemail on his way home from the party three hours ago. The call could be her. Or, since he'd left without saying goodbye—a mistake—Gabby might want to touch base. But after eleven? He paused the show he'd been streaming and plucked the phone off the coffee table.

Isabella. His breath faltered as he lifted the phone to his ear.

"You called?" Isabella never had been one to extend olive branches.

Tim rubbed his forehead. What would a good father say? Something that wouldn't alienate her further? "Were you right? Did it hurt less this way?"

She didn't reply.

"You didn't have to go, Is." He'd been about to call her Issy, so he'd stopped short. He could've still gone ahead and used her full name, but his brain had waited a second too long to chime in with that helpful tidbit.

"We're down to one syllable?"

"I'm sorry."

"Lars called me that. Is. A form of the verb 'be.'" She intoned the statement as though reading a dictionary. "As if anyone would ever like me if I were to just 'be.'"

Dull pain pulsed in Tim's temples. "*I* like you. I wanted to take this trip with you. I'm more disappointed than you'll know that it ended so badly. I wish you'd stayed."

"The whole trip was a farce. All our reasons to go—your tumor and my engagement—were resolved before we left LA, but we both knew we had nothing else to go on, so neither of us said anything. Lo and behold, the truth comes out, and what was left? It was bound to end in disaster. All I did was call it."

"That's ridiculous. I'm still your father. Love is still holding us together." Did everyone sound this corny when they shared their hearts?

"Like it held me and Mom together?"

Isabella had lived with her mom until age fourteen, when her mom remarried. At that point, his ex had insisted Tim take custody. No wonder Isabella had fled Many Oaks upon learning Gabby and Tim were making plans together.

If only he could look her in the eye to make sure she understood. "I'm so sorry, Isabella. You and Charity asked me to go out with her, so I thought you were okay with it. But you probably just had a few dates in mind, not a future. I never considered your experience with your mom."

"It's fine." She sniffled. "It's how the world works."

"Abandonment isn't supposed to be the norm." He waited, but she didn't reply. "Regardless of any other relationship, you'll always be important to me, and I'm going to prove it."

"How?" Breathy and quiet, Isabella's voice reminded him of when she'd been little. He'd visited for her fourth birthday and given her a little mechanical dog. When he'd told her the pup did tricks, she'd handed him the leash, which doubled as a controller, and asked the same question. He'd made quick work of showing her how to operate the toy. Then his guilt, spurred on by her mom's passive-aggressiveness, had carried him away from her. He hadn't shown up in person for a birthday again until her fourteenth.

His past strategies to connect with her had all failed. He prayed for new inspiration. He couldn't rely on surprises or omissions anymore. Nor could he allow guilt and shame to call the shots. He had to put his daughter first, no matter the cost. "Instead of relying on business to bring me to your area like I have been, I'll make special trips to New York to see you a couple of times a year. And what's a night of the week when you're usually home?"

"Um ... Tuesday?"

He switched the phone to speaker and added a weekly reminder. "Then on Tuesdays, I'm going to call you to check in. No more waiting for something to go wrong."

"I'm not free every Tuesday."

"That's fine. I'll leave a message." He switched off speaker, finally feeling confident that he could come through for Isabella in ways that mattered. "But when we do run into problems, let's face them. Together. No keeping secrets or guessing at solutions or running away. Deal?"

"Are you sure that's going to ... work?"

"I'm sure what we've been doing *hasn't* been working. I'll stick with this new plan. I need you to, too."

"Okay." Despite a wobble of uncertainty, she sounded hopeful.

Tim would do everything possible to ensure that hope didn't end in disappointment. "As for this trip, I'm skipping out on Million Dollar Ransom to join you in New York."

"You're leaving Many Oaks early?"

"This trip was always about you, and you're not here."

"Gabby will be disappointed."

Wouldn't be the first time. She'd looked so worried yesterday. Why hadn't he thought to tell her about his upcoming surgery sooner? At least this way, she had a taste of how poorly he navigated relationships. "I'll explain. She'll understand."

She might even be relieved to bid him good riddance. After he'd let news of his tumor sideswipe her, Gabby might've realized he was nowhere near as reliable as Judah had been.

"I'll see how early I can get there." He stood in search of his laptop. "If there's a red eye, I'll take it. Otherwise, I'll book the first one tomorrow."

"You're going to walk away from everything?"

"For the sake of my daughter? Absolutely." He flipped open the computer on the dining table and hit the button to power it up. "I'll send my flight info as soon as I have it, and I'll see you tomorrow."

"Okay. See you. Love you."

Admitting the truth about Gabby and addressing Isabella's pain hurt, but he'd suffer it a hundred times over to hear that lift of hope in Isabella's voice.

15

Waves of anticipation and melancholy alternated in washing over Gabby as she approached Tim's door. Though she brought good news of her breakthrough, tonight Million Dollar Ransom would take the stage at The Depot. Whether they impressed Tim or not, he'd leave tomorrow.

She pressed the doorbell and gripped her purse strap with both hands.

No answer. No noise.

She checked her watch. Eight-thirty might be too early to ring doorbells on Saturday mornings, but she and Tim had missed their chance to talk last night. Busy with her guests, she hadn't even realized he'd gone until ten thirty. She'd considered reaching out when she'd left The Depot at eleven, but she'd ruled it out as impolite.

So was showing up unannounced first thing in the morning, but her manners had drowned in coffee and hopes of reconciliation. She peeked beyond the front window but only discerned a couch and a curtain. Was he still sleeping? Or out already? His SUV wasn't in the drive but might be in the garage.

The front door swung open. Tim was up and dressed.

She inhaled to launch into her realizations, but Tim held up a finger. She hadn't noticed the phone at his ear.

"The seventeenth will work great." He listened to the response as he motioned Gabby inside. "Yes, you have my email?"

Must be a business call.

She stepped onto a tiled entry. To her left, a small breakfast nook flowed into the galley-style kitchen. She left her purse and wandered into the living room on her right. The owner had decorated in calming grays, white, and teal. The sunset painting over the candle-filled fireplace drew her eye with pops of yellow and coral.

"Okay. See you then." The phone clunked as Tim set it on the table. "I have news."

She turned toward him, but he stopped advancing at the edge of the living room carpet. The generous windows dominated the front wall, spilling light over him. His look of intensity seemed incongruent with the bright, airy space. A suitcase she hadn't noticed earlier stood beside the armchair.

He motioned for her to take a seat. She lowered onto the couch, concern threatening to extinguish the peace from last night's epiphanies.

He sat far enough away that they weren't touching, but close enough that they could. Potentially. If this conversation went well.

"Watching you with your daughters last night and seeing the slideshow impacted me." His hands swished as he worked them together. "I should've been there for Isabella all along, sharing life with her. That's what a father should do." He shot her a furtive glance. "It's what Judah did."

"Judah?"

"He was in the slideshow, and he must've been amazing to you and the girls for you to miss him like you do. That's a high bar. One I ... can't hope to live up to. Not overall. But with Isabella, I'm going to give it my best shot."

This struggle to measure up and get things right was sweet, if misguided. "Comparing yourself to a man you've never met is a great way to torture yourself."

He passed his hand over his chin. "Even I could see he was present. He was either in or taking a lot of the pictures in last night's slideshow."

"Maybe not as many as you think. He was a good husband. We were happy together, and I loved him, but not even he was perfect." She hesitated to continue, but she sensed Tim needed to see Judah as a whole person, not a perfect standard. "He worked full-time and coached a team. Some days we barely spent five minutes together. He pursued success so doggedly that sometimes his coaching won games and lost morale. And being raised by a pair of perfectionists wasn't easy on our daughters. I think, in their own ways, they're both afraid to fail. I'm not saying this to bash anyone. I'm just trying to assure you we're all human."

He frowned as though suppressing a counterpoint. "She and I have a plan to build a better relationship moving forward. It's not perfect, but it's something. In the meantime, this trip was supposed to be about Isabella, and it was supposed to last until Monday." With all this talk of Judah, Tim's tone reminded her of the one her late husband had used while dissecting an unexpected loss. "I need to make that happen. That was Million Dollar Ransom on the phone. I'm going to catch a show next month in Kansas City instead of tonight so I can end this trip with my daughter the way I meant to all along."

"You're leaving today?"

"In a couple of hours. You were my next call."

A phone call? She respected his choice to go after his daughter, but a phone call? Between her near panic attack at lunch yesterday and his premature departure from the party, important business remained unsettled between them.

Was there still time, or had her difficulty with his news yesterday destroyed their fragile plans? Gabby's eyes welled, and she squeezed her hands between her knees.

When Tim touched her arm, she took the unspoken invitation and leaned into him.

They'd arrived at the inevitable goodbye a day early.

FOR ALL TIM'S fears about not being good about sharing his life with another person, he could share his shoulder with Gabby forever. She rested her head there now, the weight of her hair on his T-shirt discernable only when she moved. Its scent tangled with his good sense and told him to write everything else off and stay. Except, of course, he couldn't.

Isabella was too important.

"I have a lot of hope," she said.

Hope? Really? Her tears had suggested other emotions, but he suppressed his skepticism as she sat up. Leaning into him had mussed her hair, and he ran his fingers through the soft strands, straightening it out. When he finished, he folded his hands to keep them from straying to her again.

After the worries she'd expressed yesterday, whatever hope she had might not be for a chance at a relationship with him.

"I'm sorry the slideshow discouraged you. It had the opposite effect on me." Amber-like richness infused her brown eyes, alight with something more than the sunshine. "The Lord's been good to me. The first fifty years of my life have been different from what I imagined when I set out to follow in Aunt Gladys's footsteps, but they've also held a lot of adventures."

"I'm glad." Though he meant the words, his smile felt dishonest when he wanted to get up, walk away, and spare himself the pain of being told she'd decided she didn't need him in her life. He let the false smile drop but stayed put.

Gabby bit her lower lip, her cheeks rounding with joy. "I want that to continue into however many years the Lord grants me. I'm through playing it safe. I'm pursuing the opportunities He's laid on my heart."

Her joy, combined with talk of seizing opportunities, could only amount to one thing, right? His arm twitched with the impulse to reach out to her, but he tensed and held still. "You're going to become a locum?"

Her nod jostled the waves at the ends of her hair. "That's one opportunity. The other"—she lifted her hand as though on course for his own, but paused, leaving it suspended—"unless I've scared you off, is you."

Only as his knotted muscles relaxed did he realize just how tense he'd been. He fought against clutching her in his arms and making all kinds of premature promises—when had he become so impulsive?—and instead snagged her floating hand and sandwiched it between his. "I thought *you* were scared."

"Only when I take my eyes off Jesus." She scooted closer and angled toward him so her knee pressed against his thigh. With her free hand, she traced her thumb over his wrist. "He doesn't always work the way I want, but not even death will steal the good He has in store for His people." Fingers stilling, her brown irises lifted. "I don't know exactly how that will look in my life. But as my daughters pointed out to me last night, life wouldn't be an adventure if I could see everything coming."

"So surprises aren't bad?"

Her eyes glinted, and her hands pressed into his as she tipped toward him and pressed a surprise peck on his lips. She dropped back into her place, joy creasing her temples and filling her cheeks. "*Definitely* not."

He brushed his knuckle from her temple to her chin. She'd made her choice and, amazingly, she'd picked him. He leaned in and kissed one of those happy cheeks. "Remind yourself of that when I spring one on you that you don't like."

Her breath fluttered across the inside of his wrist. This close, her irises were more intricate than the finest blown glass, but when her focus settled on his mouth, he followed suit. "This isn't the end for us?"

He kissed her first, but in case that wasn't a clear enough answer, he followed up with his voice. "*Definitely* not."

~

"Behold, I am doing a new thing;
now it springs forth, do you not perceive it?
I will make a way in the wilderness
and rivers in the desert."

— ISAIAH 43:19, ESV

A sweet small-town romance exclusively for email subscribers.

Food trailer owner Asher has seen too many tears he couldn't dry. Determined to be part of the solution, he avoids romance and all the heartbreaking drama that comes along with it.

At least, that's the plan until his heart decides it has a mind of its own. If he can't rein it in, he's destined to break not one but two women's hearts.

Sign up for email newsletters at emilyconradauthor.com and receive *Between The Two of Us*, the prequel novella to the Rhythms of Redemption Romances, as a welcome gift.

DID YOU ENJOY THIS BOOK?

Help others discover it by leaving a review on Goodreads and
the site you purchased from!

ACKNOWLEDGMENTS

Thank you, readers, for following Tim into the adventure of a new series! I appreciate all the ways you invest in these characters.

I'm also grateful to my critique partners, beta readers, and volunteer proofreaders, Jessica J., Katie, Amy, Jessica B., and Janet, Teresa, Sarah, and Maria. Robin and Judy, thank you for lending your expertise and guiding this story toward its potential.

Lord, thank You for working all things for good, even when I can't see Your plan in the moment. Please help me to keep my eyes on You.

ABOUT THE AUTHOR

Emily Conrad writes contemporary Christian romance that explores life's relevant questions. Though she likes to think some of her characters are pretty great, the ultimate hero of her stories (including the one she's living) is Jesus. She lives in Wisconsin with her husband and their energetic coonhound rescue. Learn more about her and her books at emily-conradauthor.com.

facebook.com/emilyconradauthor

twitter.com/emilyrconrad

instagram.com/emilyrconrad

9 781957 455075